www.ChloeEmile.com

# Finn

## Wild West Cowboys

Book 1

# Chloe Emile

This is a work of fiction. Names, characters, organizations,places, events, and incidents are either products of the author's imagination or are used fictitiously.

FINN
Copyright © 2015 by Chloe Emile. All rights reserved.

ISBN-13: 978-1987859232
ISBN-10: 1987859235

# CONTENTS

# CHAPTER ONE

1853, *Sedelia, Missouri*

Finn O'Cleary stood with his feet wide apart, his brown leathery hands hanging loosely at his sides. He gazed down the dirt street of Sedalia, Missouri. On either side of him were brothels and saloons.

Some of the doors were blocked by the bejeweled bodies of painted ladies, each one smiling and winking and moving her hips in various contortions, trying to seduce the twelve cowboys, which included Finn, who had finally made it safely across the Shawnee Trail despite having to run the longhorns through a gauntlet of angry farmers. Not one cowboy had been injured.

The whole scene of blatant seduction made his blue eyes widen as he heard far-off voices in his head. An isolated memory, often repeated, rolled through his mind again despite the number of times he had flung it away. The memory was of his tiny hand pulling back the burlap curtain hanging between the rooms of his family's farmhouse in Ireland.

The voices of his parents were raised in anger. A young boy of sixteen stood with his head lowered. Finn couldn't see his face. He never could remember the face of his dead brother. He had died of consumption at seventeen. He had tried to remember, but the one named after his Da was no longer even a shadow in his mind. He heard the biting words of his dear mum echoing in his head, *No son of mine is going to be fallooting with any ladies of the night. We are a family. Families are respectable, God-fearing people, Keenan O'Cleary! Go right now to Father Michael. Right now, you head for Shankill Church and fall on your knees, you hear me? Save your soul, Keenan O'Cleary!*

Finn's dirty fingertips rubbed the sweat of his brow into his. He momentarily wished he could tell his mum that no matter what happened in his life, he would not succumb. He wished he could tell her that he had listened even if his brother Keenan had not. He thought of his own hometown of Irish Flats, back in Texas, hundreds of miles away. Irish Flats was a fairly civilized town. With effort, he ran his fingers through his grimy brown hair with layers of encrusted dust from the trail.

He felt a sudden firm slap on his back.

"Whatcha waitin' for, Finn?" A familiar voice laughed heartily.

Finn turned to see his friend Patch standing behind him. Patch's face was crusted with dirt encircling his eyes and mouth. A faded red bandanna hid the layers of dirt around his neck, and the brim of his hat almost hid his dirt-rimmed black-olive eyes.

"Jus' look at the enchanting delights—"

Finn didn't let his friend finish. "Unless you are wantin' an anointing, Patch O'Riley, you will just take your kecks wherever you desire and leave me alone! I'm reading the signs, just looking for a hot bath. I know your plan is to take that bald head of yours and find yourself a lobster kettle, but I am not interested in these ladies. I aim to find a hot bath." He made a fist and punched it into the hard shoulder of his friend.

"You're jus' a baby, Finn O'Cleary. I forgot that you don't like to use that blanket hornpipe of yours. Savin' yourself for some sweetie. And don't you be talking bad about my hairless head or where I desire to take my pants!"

"If I had a hairless head like yours, I'd keep it hidden under my hat." Finn chuckled as he reached over and knocked the cowboy hat off his friend's bald head. "On second thought, I guess if I had your hairless head, I would be lookin' for my one opportunity in this town, but have no fear, Patch O'Riley. I know that with my own thick red mop washed and shining, when the time comes one day, I can have any girl I want, anytime I want, but I'm not lookin' for jus' any ol' girl, Patch O'Riley." He steadied his look on his hatless friend. "I'm lookin' for the mother of my future children."

Finn was a sincere, decent young fellow. As his boyhood friend, Patch knew that, but he didn't always understand him.

"Why you are saving yerself for a rib is beyond me!" Patch said. "Who needs a wife when there is a cornucopia jus' waitin'?" The older trail hand laughed warmly. He had always taken Finn under his protective wing, as if he was a younger brother. "I tell you, Finn Michael, it will be a sad day for girls everywhere when you enter the priesthood." His grin cracked the dirt around his mouth.

Any other time, Finn O'Cleary would have let his friend have it, but the long trail from

Irish Flats to Sedalia, Missouri had taken its toll on the young Irish lad. His stomach was already full of fighting. He truly hadn't relished fighting off those hard-working farmers along the Shawnee trail. Finn felt they had just cause to be angry.

Their mission was to take sick cattle on a drive to where the railroad ended, to put them on a train for the slaughter houses. He had just finished taking the herd through hostile Indian territory as well as hostile ranch territory because of the ranchers' anger about the dying cattle. The scare of Texas cattle fever was real for those farmers because if their own cattle got infected, they had a one-hundred-percent chance of dying.

Finn's thoughts quickly retraced the events of their trail breach with the farmers. The farmers shot at them to keep the cattle from coming onto their grazing territory. Finn had to take the cattle through their territory on the trail because it was the only way to get the cattle to market. He could still hear the bellowing of the longhorns as they spooked from all the gunshots those angry farmers shot into the air.

Some of the shots even downed a few of the steers. Unconsciously, he reached up and rubbed his ear, pushing his hat up and down on his head with each movement of his scratching fingers. *It's lucky our longhorns have a lineage of retinta, that sturdy Bakewell English and Spanish. I do believe that's what saves them from being knocked out like the not-up-to-Dick northern cattle.* He remembered rolling in the dust with a young farmer, beating on his body with his fists. "No *one wins when fighting the sons of the Irish, boy*," he had declared into the bleeding face of the prone man.

Finn's voice was low and flat. "Patch, I don't wanna shake a flannin with you. I had enough fightin' on the trail. I jus' want a bath with lots of hot water and maybe a shave and a haircut. I might even get one of those door-knocker cuts like some rich dude."

Patch's voice softened. "Sure, kid." Patch pointed at a sign scratched on a big white board, "Right there, it says Hot Baths, but promise me you ain't going to get no door-knocker face cut."

Finn's head snapped toward the sign. His grin cracked the dirt in the hollows of his cheeks. "I'll be seeing you, Patch! I got a tub waiting for me!" He jammed his boot into the dust as he turned. "Don't forget—tomorrow mornin', we head back."

Patch didn't hear Finn's warning. He had already disappeared behind one of the many establishment doors. Finn started to cross the street toward the bathhouse when he heard the distinct whinny of several horses and the clop of feet at the other end of town. He glanced toward the sound just as a stagecoach came to a halt in a cloud of brown dust in front of one of the saloons. He stopped to watch as the passengers clambered out, each one rocking the stagecoach from side to side.

A man dressed in a city suit got out first. He immediately used his hands to dust off his clothes, which was near impossible. Behind him, a white parasol pushed forward, and tiny booted feet landed in the dust, almost stepping on his. The man turned and let the woman move forward but didn't offer his hand. She kept the parasol open at her side, obstructing the view of her face, but two white gloves were holding the parasol's brass handle. She let go of the handle with one hand and with her other hand gripped her full skirt and lifted it slightly, revealing what Finn knew was one of several white lace-trimmed petticoats.

Almost instantaneously, several gunshots rang out nearby. Behind the coach, two horses reared into the air as the gun-wielding men pulled their reins to a sudden halt. The gunshots continued into the air. The city-suit man fell into the dust, covering his head with his arms. The woman's white parasol tumbled into the street, its owner's eyes wide with terror as she stood immobilized by fear.

Finn didn't think. He ran straight for her, grabbed her tiny waist, and swooped her onto the ground and quickly rolled her under the stagecoach. He was grateful the young woman wasn't wearing one of those new stiff circle hoops under her dress that so many women were adopting.

For a moment, he thought, *She's a tiny thing. Light as a feather.* He lay by her side, clutching his arm tightly around her as they watched from under the coach as the hooves of the outlaws' horses pranced back and forth beside it.

# Chapter Two

"Where's the bank in this town, Jessie?" a deep, gruff voice called out. The horse sauntered back and forth.

"Lookie there, Billie. I swear I see a white petticoat peeking out from under that stagecoach." The other horse's hooves circled the coach and stopped. The outlaws slid off his horse, and his dirty brown boots hit the ground. The young woman held her breath and prayed. She felt the man next to her pull her closer and whisper in her ear.

"Don't say a word."

She pressed her lips together tightly and stared at the approaching boots.

The second voice commanded, "Come out from under there, woman. I won't hurt you. Tell her I won't hurt her, will I, Billie?" The man seemed ready to bend down and look under the coach.

Another pair of boots walked up next to the first. "Leave her be, Jessie. We aren't here for women. We're here for the money. Plenty of time for cavorting another time. Come on."

"But, Billie, we always have time for–"

The voice rose. "Jessie, I ain't going to tell you twice. Leave 'er be." The boots turned and walked in the opposite direction. "The bank's right over there. Come on."

The street was empty. Anyone who'd heard the first shots had already hidden themselves. Jesse warned, "We don't want to wait for the sheriff to come nosing about now, do we?"

"Guaranteed, there ain't no sheriff to worry about, Billie."

Jessie had just uttered those ill-fated words when a third pair of boots joined them. "Hello, boys. Well, what the young fella jus' said is not quite true. There are two things you need to worry about in this town. One is this reliable .44 caliber Henry with its rimfire metallic cartridge. And just so's you two fellas know, this little town of Sedalia, also known by some as the Sodom and Gomorrah of the West, does indeed have a sheriff, a sheriff who downright cherishes peace. I mean, I *really* like peace. I like all the folks in my town happy, and right now it doesn't seem to be the case. Seems you fellas aren't quite understanding what peace means. I'm appointed sheriff, H.J. McCormack. Ya see, I tend to look the other way with the ladies of the night, but I draw the line at gun-slinging desperadoes." He paused to look into each of their faces. His fingers caressed the oak handle of his Henry rifle. "Pleased to meet you, boys. Sorry you'll have to be leaving my town so soon."

Finn tightened his hold on the young woman's waist when he heard the undeniable *click* of a cocked gun. The woman's gloved fingers yanked at his hand, trying to remove it. He kept his arm tightly over her but loosened his hand's grip on her waist. He couldn't see her face, but the huge rim of her bonnet pushed into his face, and her fresh scent lingered in his trail-burnt nostrils. He thought he heard a slight growl emit from her throat as she pulled her body away from him in an attempt to leave a respectable space between them.

The sheriff's voice was steady but firm. "Now, boys, why don't you just remount those horses and head out the way you came. I really don't want to use my Henry on you two handsome fellas."

Jessie shouted, "Shoot 'em, Billie! Go on an' shoot 'em."

There was another *click* and then a loud *boom*, and one outlaw's body fell to the ground. The woman under the coach gasped. She saw the wide-open dark eyes staring blankly at her under the wagon. The face was distorted by a macabre permanent grin. Fortunately, she couldn't see the ragged-edged gigantic hole in the man's chest. She started and involuntarily pushed closer toward Finn.

The other boots, belonging to the man named Billie, were gone in a few seconds, and the horses' hooves turned and were gone, too, leaving a cloud of dust that rolled under the wagon, causing the woman a coughing fit.

Finn rolled out from under the wagon and reached underneath to grab the woman's gloved hand.

She rolled out from under the stagecoach and let Finn's steady hand help her stand. She continued coughing, and then her soft pink mouth drew into a pout before she spoke. "How dare you touch me, you uncouth barbarian!"

Finn grinned. "Pleased to meet you, too. I'm Finn O'Cleary." He removed his hat and let his dusty locks fall to the middle of his forehead.

"You, sir, are *no* gentleman!" She smoothed the front of her dress with her dirt-smudged white gloves.

The sheriff sauntered to their side. "I'm so sorry that you were met by such heathens, ma'am. I am Sheriff McCormack."

She took a deep breath, pushing the memory of the dead man's blank, staring eyes out of her mind. "I am Margaret Mae Ditmar. My father is Hans Ditmar of New Braunfels, Texas. Perhaps you know of him, kind sir?" She adjusted her bonnet, but the brim was quite indented, adding a comic appearance to her dust-smudged face.

The sheriff tried not to smile. His eyes hung on the dirt clinging to the tip of her tiny button nose. The sheriff shook his head. "I can't say I know of your father, young lady, but there is a lot of land out here in the West, and Texas is an all-out world to itself. Doubt very much if I would have the opportunity to run into your daddy." He smiled warmly. "Are you traveling unaccompanied to Braunfels? I find it difficult to believe a father would ask his lovely daughter to make such a perilous journey alone."

Margaret Mae straightened her back and looked straight into the sheriff's disapproving eyes, "Sir, my father would not require me to do such a hazardous thing. I assure you, I came of my own accord from Hartford, Connecticut. I was attending Harriet Beecher Stowe's Female Seminary, studying the worthy subjects of sewing and religion. However, I felt I could better serve the needs of my widowed father if I were to come to him in Texas." She coughed into her gloved hand.

The sheriff smiled. "So your father has no idea that you are out here on this perilous journey alone?"

She glanced at Finn and stated as a firm warning, "The good Lord has protected me thus far, and I fear no evil." As if evoking the good Lord wasn't enough, Margaret Mae added, "There have always been others traveling with me. I haven't been alone." She glanced at the city-suited man who was once again dusting off his suit with his hands. "I have done quite well. I traveled by train, and then I went by steamboat down the Missouri River, which was quite an adventure, and I have just completed this part of my journey by coach from Boonville."

The sheriff glanced at Finn and then jerked his head toward him. "Miss Margaret, is this gentleman a friend of yours?" He took note that Finn was not wearing a gun.

Margaret Mae vehemently shook her head. "I do not know this man at all, nor do I choose to. I assure you, sir, he is no gentleman!" Her eyes blinked rapidly as she took in Finn's filthy hair, his dirt-caked mouth and the whiskers matted on his cheeks and chin. Her eyes lingered momentarily on his azure eyes, which seemed even brighter and larger, like two big blue saucers, because of the frame of crusted earth around them.

She turned toward the sheriff. "Sheriff, I beg of you, is there a place where a decent woman can be with other women and tend to her toiletries unabashed and without fear?"

The sheriff could no longer control his smile, the corners of his thin lips turning up swiftly. "Well, the one thing Sedalia does have is an abundance of ladies. I think I can introduce you to someone who will take good care of you, Miss Margaret."

Margaret Mae overlooked his comment that she needed to be taken care of. Her incensed thoughts raced, but she kept them from barging out of her mouth. It often was with some effort that she remained a lady. She wanted to shout, *"No one has taken care of me since I was three years old, when my* mutter *passed!"*

Her memory floated back to when she had come with her parents on the great ships to Galveston from Biebrich, Germany, which was situated on the Rhine River near Mainz. She had survived the hazardous ocean journey even though she was only three years old. Many full-bodied adults and children had died on that voyage. Her only vague memory of that time was the splashing sound she heard as their rigid bodies were dumped over the side of the ship.

Every day of the voyage, her tiny body was lifted up by her father, and she would witness the swaddled body of an *unfortunate* disappear under the waves. She would hear the familiar slosh of water as the weighted body sank. Her mother would whisper under her breath, "Oh dear poor Unfortunate, 'Yea, though I walk through the valley of the shadow of death, I will fear no evil; for Thou art with me; Thy rod and Thy staff, they comfort me.'" Margaret Mae would often strain her memory, trying desperately to see her mother's face and hear her mother's soft voice again.

As the years passed, recalling her mother's voice became more and more difficult. Sixteen years later, doing so was almost impossible. Memories were like tulle fog on a marsh—dense and cold and fading in the morning's light and warmth.

She knew the German emigrants their family had traveled with were led by the Adelsverein Society. They had been formed to protect Germans coming to Texas. *They didn't protect my mutter*, she thought defiantly. Their family had joined 4,304 other emigrants in Carlshafen, Texas and then traveled on to New Braunfels. Her father had immediately sent her away after her mother's death, a harsh and unnecessary move. Her father was all the family she had left. After he sent her away, she had no family.

Margaret looked from the sheriff's face to the face of the young Irish man. "Sheriff, would you mind escorting me to your lady friend? I don't want this Papist swine near me." She glanced over her shoulder as she took the sheriff's arm. "Can you have someone bring my valise?"

The sheriff continued to grin. "Miss Ditmar, I feel it is my duty as sheriff to point out a few things that you may not know, being as you are a newcomer and all. Things are a lot different out here, and most of us don't fancy little princess-type gals telling us what to do. Sadly, I believe you are going to learn some harsh lessons living out West. Number one lesson, people don't just hop around when someone wags their little finger at them and tells them to jump, unless, of course, that someone is holding a gun pointed at them!"

Finn stepped back to let the two of them pass in front of him. He couldn't believe that Miss Margaret would even look at him again, but of course, unbeknownst to him, she had, out of the corner of her big brown eyes.

As she stared at him, she thought, *However in the world could anyone become that soiled?* She pushed out her chin as she tilted up her head.

Finn turned and saw the body of the dead outlaw being dragged away by what he supposed was the town's undertaker. The undertaker glanced at him and then continued to drag the lifeless body by its feet through the middle of the street, leaving one deep furrow made by the outlaw's head and a wet line of black blood.

Finn shook his head, thinking, *Death... Everywhere there's death.*

Back on the trail when the farmers had attacked to spook the Texas cattle, there had also been the mantle of death. *That stupid farmer. Why did he shoot up in the air like that while he was smack in the middle of the herd? Of course the longhorns stampeded.* Finn shook his head in an attempt to erase his memory of the man's horse buckling under him. Finn saw the horror in the farmer's eyes when the farmer realized what was happening. The farmer's eyes were frozen, like two black pebbles, as he faced his own imminent death.

Finn's thoughts returned to the present. The sheriff stopped walking in the middle of the road and turned toward Finn. He raised his voice slightly so it would carry. "Sir, could you ever so kindly deliver Miss Margaret's valise to the hotel?" The sheriff pointed to a building across the street. Before Finn could protest, the sheriff placed his fingers over Margaret Mae's white gloved hand, which was tightly clutching his bent elbow. The two began to walk again toward the hotel.

Finn heard the tinkle of her laugh. Obviously, she was amused at something Sheriff McCormick had confided in her. He thought, *What could an idiot sheriff say that would amuse such a refined young woman like Margaret Mae Ditmar?*

Finn glanced at the eight-inch barrel of a New Army gun that lay forgotten in the dust next to the stagecoach. He'd heard the cock of a gun right before the renegade was shot, but it wasn't that gun he had heard. If that unfortunate fool named Jessie had successfully cocked that gun, the fool would have had six rounds of shots, and he would have unloaded all of them into the sheriff's chest if he was a good shot. The sheriff surely would have been dead, but there he was, walking Miss Margaret Mae Ditmar toward the town's hotel, certainly not dead.

Finn leaned over and picked up the gun. He stared at it a moment, marveling at how balanced it felt in his hand. The one-piece walnut grip was smooth and shiny.

*Yep, had that renegade bank robber ignited this percussion cap, this gun would have happily taken that fulminate of mercury and exploded smack in that sheriff's chest. The man wouldn't have had a chance even to say his last Our Father.* Finn shoved the muzzle into the waistband of his kecks, the cold barrel touching the top of his leg, the grip caught tightly by his suspenders.

"Imagine finding a gun," he said aloud, strolling toward the bathhouse and ignoring the sheriff's orders to deliver the valise to prissy Miss Margaret. He glanced to the right and saw the open white parasol poised and forgotten in the dust.

# CHAPTER THREE

Patch was up with the sun. He had breakfast and then sat leisurely outside the hotel, sniffing the fresh morning air. He smiled ear to ear when he saw Finn leaving the hotel. Finn's washed brown hair sparkled a reddish copper in the morning's light. He wore a fresh bleached cotton shirt pulled tightly over his muscled chest. Devoid of the trail's dust, he looked downright human again, if not like a gentleman. Patch, too, was no longer encrusted in dirt. Patch grinned as he thought, It's *amazing what a little soap can do for a man!*

"Been waiting long, Patch?" Finn's smile lit up his blue eyes with a rested mischievousness.

"Nope. Had some bags o' mystery with a couple of eggs, washed it all down with strong hot coffee, and…" He studied Finn's clean-shaven face. "What? No door-knocker?"

"No, not my style."

Patch laughed. "Now the city boy is talkin' about style? So, had a good night, did you?"

Finn answered, "Uneventful. And you?"

"*Very* eventful." Patch laughed again. "You, boy, have so much to learn."

Finn shook his head. "Well, Patch, I figure you have what, ten years on me? I have plenty of time to learn what you think is going to get me through life."

"Oh, not just get you through life, my dear oblivious one, but enjoying life!" The cowpoke sighed.

"I enjoyed my hot bath, and when I shake my head, it doesn't feel like I have weighted rope tied to it. I can actually take my hand and run it through my hair and not get my fingers stuck in it. That's downright enjoyment enough for me, Patch. Had a soft bed, too. I almost had to get up and lay on the floor 'cause it was just too soft." Finn's smile unwrapped shining-white teeth. "Shall we begin the trek back to Texas, my friend?"

Patch shook his head. "Hate to, but got to. Winter's licking its chops. Took almost a hundred days getting here, but I reckon we can make it back in forty or so without the cattle." He took his hat off and let it hang loosely in front of him. "I kind of like this little town."

"Let's face it, Patch. You like what is *in* this little town." Finn reached down and patted the cowboy's bald head. "Come on. Bring this hairless boulder, and let's hit the trail."

"Wouldn't you like to hit the trail a bit half rats?" Patch grabbed Finn's arm as he turned. "There's the saloon just calling our names!"

"Ah, come on, you know I don't drink. Come on, Patch. It's too early in the morning for you to begin drinking. Let's get going. Time to say goodbye." He stepped off the wooden porch just as Sheriff McCormick came toward him.

"I was hoping to catch you boys before you left," the sheriff said. "I would have been here earlier, but we had to give that outlaw his dirt bath. That plot on the outskirts of town is getting plenty full of his types." He shook his head. "They just keep comin' to town, and I jus' keep putting them out there for their eternal rest." He lowered his voice. "Thing is, boys, I have a favor to ask of you."

"What do you need, Sheriff?" Finn asked as he thought about how lucky he was that the sheriff didn't chastise him for not bringing Miss Margaret's valise to the hotel.

The sheriff looked at Patch and then spoke directly to Finn, "Well, mainly my business has to do with you, but since the two of you seem to be partners..."

Patch nodded. "We traveled a lot of miles together, but we are two of twelve, ya know. We are all headed back together this morning."

The sheriff's thin lips inched into a smile. "That's what I figured. Well, I thought, if it wouldn't be too much trouble, that you could accompany Miss Ditmar to her home in New Braunfels, Texas. She has money to pay you."

Finn swallowed. "Sheriff, I don't think that is a wise decision. You heard Patch. There are twelve of us. That's a lot of men and only one unaccompanied lady."

"Precisely. This one lady needs to be escorted safely on the Shawnee Trail, safely to her father. Twelve able-bodied men should be able to get her to him. I am sure he will add a bonus to your wages when she is delivered to him unharmed." The sheriff unconsciously lifted his gun into the air as he spoke his last word.

The two cowboys shook their heads.

"Girls are a Jonah on a ship, ya know." Patch kept shaking his head. "I'm sure they are worse bad luck on the trail."

Finn agreed. "Much worse. It's like that French word, you know... What's the word, Patch?"

"You're asking me? You're the learned one, Finn. Doesn't Finn mean 'bright' and O'Cleary means 'learned'?"

"It means like 'bright light,' not like 'smart.' Bright and fair, but what's in a name?" He squirmed under the sheriff's stern gaze.

The sheriff shook his head. "You boys are referring to femme fatales—those Greek and Roman voices that lured ships to wreck, right? I assure you that Miss Ditmar certainly is not like the daughters of Phorcys. I promise you, she will tend to her own needs and be no trouble. If anything, she will keep her distance from the likes of all of you. The young lady just needs safe passage on the Shawnee Trail to her father's safekeeping."

Finn shook his head again, and his voice lowered with suspicion. "I heard that her father didn't send for her and he doesn't even know that she is coming."

"More's the reason she needs protection. She obviously is an empty-headed girl. What girl with any amount of brain would go against her father's wishes? I have three daughters of my own, and I would like to think that their safety would be the paramount concern of decent young men such as yourselves." The sheriff's fingers moved slightly on the handle of his gun. "This town is no place for a young lady of such refined stature such as Miss Ditmar. Left here in this town, she would only succumb to..." The sheriff stopped, a true look of fear in the man's eyes. As if he needed to explain, he added, "I keep my own daughters far off from here on my ranch, far away from this city of sin."

Finn licked his lower lip before he asked, "Why do you trust us, Sheriff?"

"I know a God-fearing man when I see 'im, sir." His eyes met Finn's. "You are an honorable man, and I believe you will ensure that this young woman ends up in the protective arms of her father."

There wasn't much else to say. An armed sheriff was making a request, and that was that. Margaret Mae Ditmar would get her escort to Texas.

# CHAPTER FOUR

Margaret Mae glowered at the two cowboys and then turned her head toward the sheriff. "Sheriff McCormack, I do believe you have your heart in the right place, desiring me to be accompanied on my journey to my father. However, sending me with these hoodlums is, I dare say, not the solution! Dear sir, it is a breach of your judgment."

The sheriff took her by the elbow, "Listen to me, Miss Ditmar, the Shawnee Trail is named after an Indian tribe. That alone should give you fair warning. Besides, the farmers are up in arms over that Texas red-water fever killing their cattle. They are apt to shoot at anything that moves in their grasslands. Not to mention that there is a state of unrest within our great nation. Why, there are Paiute wars in Utah, and I hear that there is trouble on the Pease River in Texas with those redskins there. It just is not safe out there. It's a good forty days of riding with these men." He emphasized the word "men." "That's a 'trepid long ride for any woman to endure, even you, Miss Ditmar."

She smiled her sweetest smile and patted her freshly laundered white glove on his hand. "My dear sheriff, you worry just like a father would." Her dark cocoa eyes blinked. "I shan't need these gentlemen to escort me. I will find a stagecoach headed in that precise direction and—"

The sheriff abruptly interrupted her. "There is no stagecoach, Miss Ditmar. As it is, you shall have to travel by horse. You do know how to ride a horse, do you not?"

She gulped audibly as she swallowed. "I'm afraid not. At Miss Beecher's school, we were not offered the sport of riding. There actually weren't any horses provided. I mean, it would have been difficult... Girls just didn't..." She stopped speaking.

Patch began to laugh. "I've been watching this little charade long enough." He stabbed his elbow into Finn's ribs. "That settles it, then. Miss Ditmar won't be able to travel with us after all—more's the pity, right, Finn?"

Finn didn't speak but stared at the bewildered young woman. Her eyes darted from the face of the sheriff to each of their faces. She took a gasp of air.

The sheriff shook his head. "Don't worry, Miss Ditmar, I am sure these two cowboys can find a suitable mule to transport you to Texas. A mule will be much easier for you to ride and, of course, is closer to the ground should you unfortunately tumble off. It won't be as comfortable as a sure-footed horse, but you will have a dependable, sturdy ride. The important thing is to get started, to get back to your father before the autumn rains. I dare say the rains have already commenced in some parts."

She didn't speak, but her mouth was open in shock.

Finn repeated and unleashed the word that was frozen in her mind, "Mule?"

The sheriff nodded. "There are a few of them up for sale over at Tom Sweeny's ranch. I'll have him bring a couple round for you boys to look over."

Finn repeated, "A mule?"

The sheriff nodded again. "But I actually suggest two mules. Kind of like you boys do with your crew's remuda. A remuda is such a great idea of keeping horses always fresh for you cowboys. It just makes sense and keeps things moving swifter. Of course, Miss Ditmar won't have a remuda of six to ten horses to choose from each morning, like you cowpokes have. She'll just have her two mules to switch out, but I think it's definitely better 'n just one, especially since she can't ride a horse. If something should happen to one of the mules, at least she has the other one to rely on. I'm jus' saying. You boys probably know better."

Margaret Mae stamped her foot on the wooden porch. "I will not travel by mule, not one mule and certainly not two mules! Furthermore, I refuse to travel with the likes of these two filthy cowboys."

The sheriff's eyes twinkled. "Oh, my dear Miss Ditmar, you will not be traveling with just these two delightful gentlemen. You will be traveling with ten other gentlemen just as delightful, as well. You see, their trail crew will be traveling back to Texas together. I whole-heartedly approve as there is definitely safety in numbers and it won't cost you a penny more for all this extra vital protection. In my humble opinion, Miss Ditmar, it is a true godsend."

Finn and Patch watched Margaret Mae's face turn a bright crimson. She snorted, most unladylike through her nose, and once again stomped her foot on the wooden planks of the porch.

She moved so swiftly that her plumed and feathered bonnet jilted back and forth on her head, which in turn loosed the curls she had so carefully hidden under it. Her eyes narrowed as she reached for the porch post to steady herself in her anger. "I will not, cannot, most assuredly will not ride a mule to Texas accompanied by twelve unbridled rookery-born men who will undoubtedly take the first opportunity to commit outrage!" She spoke so passionately that tears filled her eyes. Her eyes appeared as if they were composed of melted chocolate.

Finn stepped forward with his hat in hand. His voice was calm, yet commanding. "You will be safe, Miss Ditmar. I will guarantee you safe passage to your father." After he had said it, he couldn't believe it had come out of his mouth.

She stopped ranting and stared at the cowboy in front of her. Her eyes slid over his clean clothes and lingered approvingly on his clean-shaved face and cut, groomed shiny hair. He barely resembled the young man who had attempted to save her from the marauding bank robbers.

When she didn't answer him, he added, "I'll bring the mules by the hotel for you, and then you can make your decision to go or to stay."

He nodded to Patch, and the two of them jumped off the porch. The sheriff's eyes considered Margaret Mae as he mumbled softly under his breath, "I wonder what th' heck she's gonna do next?"

She reached up her long finger and pushed an escaped light-brown curl under the confines of her bonnet. She turned and studied the two silhouettes of the men striding down the long, dusty main road of town. Finn towered over Patch though he was barely five foot eleven. Margaret sniffed haughtily and asked, "Shall I have to pay all twelve of them, then, Sheriff?" She didn't turn to look at the sheriff as she spoke.

The sheriff was startled. "Why, no... uh, of course not! Whatever wage you deem fair. However, may I suggest thirty dollars for each of them, which is a usual cowhand's fee for cattle driving?" He regretted saying it the moment it came out of his mouth.

She scowled. Her forehead wrinkled, and her eyes darkened fiercely. She reached down and snatched at her gown, pulling it up so she could move away swiftly. Her voice frosted the hot, humid air around her with ice. "Pray let me know when my mules have arrived. I will be in the hotel lobby." She turned, and her skirt swished past the sheriff, brushing against his legs as she disappeared into the hotel lobby.

Sheriff McCormack shook his head slowly. "Nope, no one's going to tinker with that one. Guaranteed." He chuckled. "I hope my daughters grow up to be exactly like Miss Margaret Mae Ditmar."

The two cowboys mounted their horses for the ride to check out the mules for Margaret Mae. They weren't about to waste more time waiting for Sweeny to bring the mules to town to them. Finn's thoughts raced. *What are we going to do with a female on the trail?* The thought almost made him shiver. *I'd rather face a bear than deal with that woman out there every day!* Sinister thoughts began to run through his mind. *We could leave her on the side of the trail. What's to say that she didn't fall off her mule when we weren't looking, and we just kept traveling and then realized she was gone?* He glanced at Patch, thankful his friend couldn't hear his thoughts, bordering on evil. "What do you think about taking this girl, Patch?"

Patch spat out a wad of tobacco, his newfound habit. "I think you and I keep most of the money. The others can just ride on ahead at their own faster pace, and we keep the money for ourselves since it's going to be us guarding the girl anyhow. The others don't even have to know. We can stall and let them all go ahead of us." His eyes locked onto Finn's. "That's what I think."

"But, Patch, don't you think this gal is going to be more trouble than she's worth? I mean, I don't believe any amount of money is going to be worth the headaches we are going to have to face if we go dragging her along with us." Finn shook his head. He pulled on the reins of his horse and came to a complete stop. He rested his hand on the saddle horn. "You know, Patch, I do believe that sheriff's got it in for us for some reason. He knows that we can't handle her. Heck, *he* can't even handle her. She's like some wild prairie mare, and no amount of attempts at taming is going to break that filly."

Patch nodded. "Well, my friend, I'd say you have your work cut out for you. This gal is definitely going to make you or break you." He grinned. "It's going to be very interesting, to say the least! That gal has one goal, and it is to get back to her daddy. I've been thinking. Why do you think her father sent her away?"

Finn's eyes momentarily lost their luster. "Sometimes there's just too much pain." He sucked in the hot humid air. "Like when I lost my mum. I still feel it, right here." Finn thumped his chest. "At first we all hated Carlin. She died giving him life." He shook his head. "Never made much sense to me and my brothers why God saw fit to take her."

Patch nodded. "How could it make sense? You were all too young."

"Death never makes sense to the living. But the thing is, in time, we came to love that little guy. I think he is the best of the five of us." Finn's eyes sparkled and reflected the blue sky once again. "He's a special fella, you know. Makes us all realize why mom wanted to name him Little Champion. Carlin James." He was silent a moment. "Mum's been gone ne'r twenty years now." He bit his lower lip. "I understand family roots. I understand Miss Margaret wanting to set out to be with her da. I'm going to help her get there. I'm going to do it, Patch. Come hell or high water, I'm going to get that gal to the arms of her da."

"But, Finn, she's such an annoying little easterner with her bothersome, snooty, city-folk habits." Patch couldn't say what he really thought. Finn didn't take much to bad language.

Finn's head bobbed up and down. "Goes to show what sending a girl to one of those eastern finishing schools can cause. Those schools create a female that is so riling that no man would ever want to even think of even considering to be her partner. She just turns a man's stomach inside out—that's what she does. I agree with you, Patch. She's downright obnoxious." He spurred the horse to move. Neither of them spoke again until they reached Sweeny's farm.

# CHAPTER FIVE

Finn held tightly to the molly mules' reins. On the way back to town, he had plenty of time to make an assessment of the two mules. His mind checked off important points that he could recount to Miss Ditmar if she desired to learn, which he thought doubtful. *I can see that the animals are indeed sure-footed. The girls keep up with my horse, so they are also faster than I expected.*

The farmer had explained to him about the mules having an estrus cycle and had called these two short, medium-weight—about eight hundred pounds—female mules mollies. Either of them could carry almost three hundred pounds if it had to. *No way are we letting that eastern woman talk us into putting three* hundred pounds of her gear on these mules! The farmer had offered them the john mules, but both he and Patch felt Miss Ditmar would object to riding a male mule. Finn smiled at that thought.

He slid off his saddle and was at once staring into the eyes of Miss Ditmar. She was sitting on the bench on the porch of the hotel, her hands politely folded in her lap. Her cocoa-brown eyes stared at him. He felt a bolt of electricity, and he looked away. She finally stood and gathered her full skirt in her two hands.

"Mr. O'Cleary, I see you have brought my mules." Her voice was steady. She sauntered over to him with her eyes fixed on the two mules. She reached out one ungloved hand and touched one of the mules' necks, which was the first time Finn had seen her naked fingers. Her fingers were long and slender, with delicate rounded points of smooth, manicured nails.

She observed the mule's short, thick head, its long ears and small, narrow hooves. "He appears to be a surprising animal. I mean, he seems like a sturdy animal." She glanced quickly at Finn and then patted the mule's neck again.

"She, not he. They are *shes*. Molly mules. I assure you, Miss Ditmar, that she has inherited her intelligence, steady gait, and her ability to endure from her sire. She indeed has superior cognitive abilities."

Margaret Mae didn't question him. She ran her fingers over the mule's long ears and short mane. "It is extremely obvious that this is unquestionably a fine strong animal." She paused to rest her hand on the mule's back. "I do believe I will be able to mount her unassisted due to her short stature." She patted the molly mule's back. She discerned that no dust rose with her patting. The mules had obviously been scrubbed clean for her.

She turned to walk behind the mule, and Finn sternly said, "I wouldn't!"

She immediately stopped. "You wouldn't what?"

"I wouldn't walk behind her. I don't believe mules like people passing closely behind their hindquarters."

She shrugged her lace-ruffled shoulders. "She seems docile enough to me." She had no sooner said this than the mule kicked out one leg, and its hoof brushed into Margaret Mae's full skirt. "Heavens!" She exclaimed as she jumped back.

"Warned you." Finn grinned. "And a word of extra caution—sometimes mules bite."

Her initial calm reaction to her new trail mate was now tampered with caution. "Indeed? I shall avoid her posterior and her obverse, judiciously." She glanced at Finn from under her feather-topped bonnet.

Finn thought, *And some bird gave his all for that bonnet, I dare say.* He carried a saddle to the mule, flipped it up on the mule's back, and adjusted it. As he checked the cinches, he spoke softly, more for Miss Ditmar than for the mule. "You'll find that she is quite enduring and patient. She won't mind your weight or a few of your things loaded on her back. That's why I got you two, just like the sheriff said. Your own private remuda." He had emphasized the word "few" but doubted that Miss Ditmar was listening. In his head, he began to practice phrases such as *Yes, Miss Ditmar* and *No, Miss Ditmar. I am not going to get familiar with you at all, Miss Ditmar!*

He continued to educate her about her new mode of transportation. "A mule's skin is really tough. Tougher than horses. She's going to withstand the rains and the beating sun." He tried to peek under Miss Ditmar's sombrero. She might call it a bonnet, but where he came from, any hat that big with a brim that wide was called a sombrero.

Of course, he'd never seen a sombrero with wild bird feathers trying so dreadfully unsuccessfully to fly off the top of it! He couldn't see her eyes, which in retrospect might have been a blessing. *Is she even listening to me?* He wanted to add, *These mules are going to do much better 'n you out there in the sun and rain, that's for sure.* But he didn't. He continued, "Her hooves are tough, too. She's going to be a nice, steady ride for you, Miss Ditmar."

Miss Ditmar didn't respond to a single thing he told her.

"May I ride sidesaddle?" she asked as she gingerly touched the stirrup.

Finn thought for a long moment before he answered her. "I got you a nice saddle tree, but you have to ride like a cowboy. It's bull hide over beechwood. That's the best." He paused, waiting for her to acknowledge or thank him for purchasing her the best saddle, but of course she didn't say a word. "You even have a horn that's decent, 'cept you won't snub a lariat since you won't be roping any cattle." He stopped as he began to feel a bit foolish. She tilted her head back, and he could plainly see her liquid brown eyes staring at him. "I got you the flat seat so your legs will be under you to help keep your balance."

She sniffed and tilted her head even higher. "I dare say you should not be discussing my legs so blatantly, Mr. O'Cleary."

He felt his face burning, but he continued. "Those are Tapadaros stirrups with one-hundred-percent wool cinches, and you can tie your gear with those saddle strings." He ran his hand along the back of his neck nervously. "And there's britching to keep your saddle from moving forward. You know mules tend to have narrow shoulders, and..."

She had turned toward the mule, and he watched as her two fingers lifted the stirrup in the air for her inspection. She let it drop against the mule's side.

As if she would be thrilled, he added, "And there's even a pannier to carry your goods on the other mule, and I bought you the finest soogan I could find for your bedroll."

He seemed to have ignited a prairie fire under her skirt. She snapped her body toward him, and her eyes became brown darts branding him to his core. "There shall be no more talk of my legs nor any other parts of my person, nor certainly not of my bedroll. Is that perfectly clear? I shall require several blankets to hang on the trees each evening for my privacy. I will travel on my own with you behind me to ensure my safety and Mister O'Riley at the front to guide the way, but other than that, we shall have no reason whatsoever to engage in even the most polite of conversations." She paused to glare at him. "Have I ensured that you are *au fait*?"

He didn't mean to, but he shook his head, trying to figure out what au fait meant. *There aren't many trees on the prairie to hang her darn blankets, but if I tell her, she'd just swallow my head*, he thought. *She'll find out soon enough. She can just darn well figure out her own solutions! Au fait! Au fait! What th' heck!*

"Mr. O'Cleary, I don't know how I can make you any more knowledgeable than I already have. It is quite simple, but I shall reiterate. Then, you most assuredly will become *au fait*. I shall endure the presence of you and the others for as long as it takes to get to my father, but I don't desire to fraternize with any of you in any shape or manner for my entire journey."

He was blunt. "What about your meals?"

"I shall take them alone." She coughed politely. "And I shall pay you half your wages now and half when I am delivered safely to my father. I am sure my father will also see fit to compensate you further."

Under his breath, Finn grumbled, "There won't be need for that."

She shrugged her small shoulders and turned to face him, her cage crinoline swaying out. "Are we to depart soon?"

He shifted from one foot to the other nervously. He lifted his hand up to his hat, which he pushed back from his eyes. "Miss Ditmar, you shan't be able to wear that hoop on the trail. I was even going to suggest that you purchase the smallest of cowboy's attire."

"Men's kecks! You want me to wear men's pants!" Her voice registered with horror. "Sir, now you truly go too far! I will not dress in a man's attire! Sir, you have breached beyond the pale."

He nodded and said slowly, "I suspect I have. But at the very least, Miss Ditmar, no hoop. I dare say even you cannot ride a mule with a hoop under your dress."

She shook her head and turned to walk away. She mumbled, "I am assuming we leave within the hour."

He watched her and her wide dress hoop disappear through the hotel's front doors before he could answer. He heard laughter behind him and turned to see the sheriff.

"She's really somethin', isn't she, boy?" The lawman continued to chuckle. "Nice lookin' mules."

Finn kicked up a poof of dust. If he had ever wanted to cuss, it was at that very moment, but he heard her voice once again, that soft melodic voice of his mum, "*Families are respectable, God-fearing people.*" But Mum, *whom does Miss Margaret Mae Ditmar fear? Is Miss Ditmar a God-fearing woman?* As if in answer, a mule let out a whinny ending in a long *heeeee-haaaaw.*

Finn threw his arms up in the air in exasperation. "Tarnation! Even the mule thinks it's funny!" He fell into the wooden seat on the porch to wait for Miss Ditmar's emergence. He thought, *Patch is the smart one, going for one last drink before we hit the trail.* He would sometimes take a sip of whiskey at dinner with his da, but Finn wasn't into drinking. He had seen too many men succumb to the evil depths of despair, losing all they loved and cared about, their wife, their children, their very lives. *No matter how miserable I get, I will just work it through, Lord, that I promise. I will just bite the bit and work it through.*

He watched the sheriff walking slowly down the dusty road. The man was no Marshall Hickok, but Finn admired him. It struck him that the sheriff's back was totally exposed to any brigand's bullet. The thought made him keenly aware of the New Army gun tucked snugly in his waist. He hadn't used a gun on a human before. Fact was, he had never really shot a gun like that one. Da had trained him with a shotgun, but that instrument was different. That morning, he had purchased some cartridges and thought about going to the outskirts of town to practice shooting.

*Thoughts never are doing,* he told himself.

He argued with himself, *Never going to have to use a gun anyhow.* Still, he wished he had at least tried shooting it a few times before hitting the trail. *My rope's always been enough,* he thought. *Cowboys just need a good sturdy rope.*

He placed his hand on the Colt .44's smooth grip. He had loaded its six-shot cylinder just that morning. *I never needed a gun before,* he thought. *Probably never need one.* He pulled it out of his waistband and laid it across his lap. His sapphire eyes narrowed as the sheriff almost reached the end of the road. *Yep, that sheriff needs someone to watch his back.* But he knew he was denying his real thoughts. *Miss Margaret Mae Ditmar needs a man with a gun if she is going to traverse the Shawnee Trail.*

Finn took a deep breath and said aloud, "I'm that man." His trigger finger slipped inside the trigger guard. He moved his finger back and forth, feeling the smooth loop of the trigger guard under the tip of his finger.

A new feeling was running through his veins. He felt it deep and strong and let it overtake him. He felt his mouth desiccating. He stood up slowly and placed the Colt back into his kecks' waistband. *I need a proper gun belt*, he thought. His boots hit the wooden deck with force and determination as he headed for the gunsmith's shop for the second time that morning. He knew what he wanted.

As soon as the gunsmith looked up, Finn blurted, "Double-drop loop with a military throat and a closed-toe holster."

The gunsmith nodded. "Sure 'nuff. Got one right here."

# CHAPTER SIX

Finn was very much aware and thankful that the woman had removed her hoop, but the hem of her dress dragged overabundantly in the dirt, which most certainly would be an impediment to her walking safely. Margaret Mae poised her foot in the stirrup and hoisted herself up onto the mule's back. She quickly bunched all the fabric of her gown around her, tucking the edges in as neatly as she could. Once she was atop the mule, she took the reins in one hand and presented a book in her other. Imprinted on its cover was the title *Song of Hiawatha*. She had tied several books wrapped in an oilskin bag with the saddle strings alongside her saddle.

Once perched on the brawny mule, she adjusted her bonnet, which seemed to have the widest brim she'd sported since Finn met her. "I am quite ready, Mr. O'Cleary."

He glared at her. "Well, Miss Ditmar, I am not." He growled. She brought out the most unpleasant in him. *Where is Patch?* he thought. As if summoned by thought, the wrangler appeared with a grin on his face. Obviously, Patch had enjoyed a few imbibements before departure. "Are you quite ready, Mr. O'Riley?"

Patch swayed to the right, and then he swayed to the left. A loud hiccup rolled from his open mouth. "I do believe I am, Mr. O'Cleary!"

Margaret Mae had already turned her mule and was headed down the street, needing no escort to find her way out of town. She lifted her ungloved hand to wave briefly at the sheriff standing at the edge of town.

He waved back, his usual wide grin commanding his face. "You take care now, Miss Ditmar," he hollered at her.

She ignored him as she turned the page of her book.

Finn turned to his friend and helped him onto his horse. "The others left earlier this morning. This is it, then, Patch. We are the official trail nannies of Miss Margaret Mae Ditmar."

Patch fell forward on his horse's neck as he shouted, "Tally ho!" Then, he began to snore. Finn tied his friend to his saddle, grabbed that horse's reins, and held them while he mounted his own. He spurred his mount to catch up with Miss Ditmar and stayed several yards behind her. Her brown locks bounced and blew in the wind from under her bonnet, and he thought he could smell her vanilla perfume riding on the breeze, even from that far back.

His thoughts hammered at him. "Who in the heck is Hiawatha?" he asked aloud, even though no one could hear him. The other ten cowboys had gone on ahead, just as Patch had thought they should. The three of them wound along the flat trail headed toward Preston, Texas, at Rock Bluff. He watched Miss Ditmar swaying back and forth on the little mule and thought, *I only hope the Red River isn't too rough yet so that we can cross. That darn ferry isn't that reliable.*

As if she could read his thoughts, Miss Ditmar turned in her saddle toward him and stopped her mule. "Mr. O'Cleary, when do we ford the first river?"

He got off his horse and strode up to her. "There are going to be a few rivers, Miss Ditmar, some of them more dangerous than others. We're headed for Indian Territory now. We are thinking that it shouldn't be too dangerous. We just have to keep going. Eventually, we will make it to the Texas border. It will be there that we will have to take Colbert's Ferry. I don't believe there is anywhere else we can cross that Red River safely at this time of year." He patted the nose of the mule. "We'll have to stop before dark. Hopefully, we'll reach a rest station."

She seemed to sit up even straighter in her saddle. "I am not tired, Mr. O'Cleary. We have barely begun." As an afterthought, she added, "So, in your estimates, sir, will we be in danger in the Indian Territory?"

He didn't want to frighten her, but he knew she had a right to know the truth. "The only Indians we have to worry about are the Comanche. Their raiding parties could be anywhere. That bunch is downright unpredictable." He watched her face for any sign of fear, but she didn't even flinch. "There are peaceful Indians, too, like the Penateka, the Caddo, and the Delaware." He omitted—quite prudently, he thought—telling her about the Tonkawa. If he explained their cannibalistic tendencies, she might have had a vapors fit. He had heard about women succumbing to attacks of the vapors. However, he observed that she didn't seem to be the least bit upset with the news that they were in Indian Territory. "We've been on the trail eight hours, Miss Ditmar. That's a long time in the saddle without a break. Perhaps we shall look for a camp for the night."

She nodded and began to lift her leg to get off of her mule. She caught her leg halfway, resting it on the mule's rump. "I seem to have become quite stiff." Her eyes caught his.

"Let me assist you." He reached around her waist and lifted her off the mule's back. Margaret Mae could feel the firm fingers squeezing her waist as Finn lifted her up and over the mule. Finn's eyes were locked on hers. Neither her eyes nor his blinked. He held her waist for a moment, until he was sure she was steady on her feet. He let his hands fall to his sides, but his blue eyes never left her brown ones. "Steady now?" he asked in a whisper.

She nodded. Her brown eyes finally blinked. "What does a girl have to do to get a cup of water around here?"

He reached for his canteen. "Truth is, Miss Ditmar, whiskey's safer than water in these parts, but I brought a couple of water canteens from Sedalia." He reached out and handed her the canteen. He assured her, "I haven't drunk from it."

"I didn't suspect you would have, giving it to a lady as you are." She placed it against her lips and tilted her head so far back that her bonnet fell off her head into the dust. He reached down quickly to retrieve it. He held it out in front of him while she finished drinking. Not until she was completely satiated did she reach for the bonnet.

She offered a brief explanation. "I loosed it while riding and forgot to tie it up again." She hobbled over to a fallen log. "Walking has become quite the challenge." She sat on the log, smoothing out her long skirt, the length of which had just dragged in the dirt. Without the hoop, the dress was much too long. She lifted the hem to inspect it and found its original color was covered eight inches up with the red dust of the trail.

"I could cut the hem for you," he offered.

"Cut my dress?" She was horrified.

"Just above the hem so that you can walk unencumbered."

"I shall manage." She sniffed into the air.

He turned away from her. He wasn't in the mood for Miss Margaret Mae Ditmar's snobbish eastern airs. His back hurt, and he still had to get a fire going and catch something for supper.

Patch had finally come out of his alcohol fog. He slid off his horse and came immediately to their side. "Something wrong here? Why are we stopped? We have another hour at least of daylight."

Finn shook his head. "Nothin's wrong. We are stopping to make camp for the night."

Patch looked around him. "Here? Can't we go a few hours to a decent rest stop? You're going to camp right here in the middle of the trail?"

"There." Finn pointed to a flat area a few feet from the trail, protected on one side by a small hill. "It will do."

Patch shrugged his shoulders. "Okay. But if you ask me—and you aren't, but if you were—we are stoppin' too early, and this isn't exactly a choice position that I would have made." He glanced at Miss Ditmar and frowned. "I'll gather some wood for a fire. If I see anything good to eat, I'll be sure to bring it back, too." He grinned. "Not much to eat around here. If we're lucky, we'll find a deer, but chances are, with our luck, it will be a rabbit or two." He headed out toward some scrub bushes. He turned and spoke again, "Keep an eye out for Comanche, Finn. We entered Indian Territory a short while back. I know it belongs to the Cherokees and Choctaw, but the Comanche is their enemy, and..." He stopped to stare at Miss Ditmar sitting on the log. "Those redskins take to white women." He grinned. "Pretty or not."

Finn patted the gun hanging on its new gun belt at his waist. "I have my eyes open."

Miss Ditmar stood up quickly. "What did he mean that they take to white women? Will they attack? Should I be worried?"

Finn wanted to tell her not to worry her pretty, curly head, but she would have just shot her dagger eyes at him. "Just means we have to be careful. There generally aren't any Comanche out this way, but Patch is just saying that we have to be careful. Could be a few renegade strays."

She undid the ribbon around her neck and laid the bonnet on the log next to her as she sat back down. "Mr. O'Cleary, I just ask that you give me fair warning if we are in peril." She smoothed her hands on her lap. "I have an entitlement to know."

Finn thought, *Entitlement indeed, you gilded canary!* However, he had to admit she was right—he had a duty to be truthful with her. "The Indians around here are the peaceful Penateka, Caddo and Delaware, and usually the Tonkawa, but the truth is, they have a tendency to be cannibals when it comes to their enemies."

She shrieked, "Cannibals! You mean that those vile creatures actually consume human beings?"

"That's what cannibals do. They eat other humans. That's why the Comanche and them fight all the time. The Tonkawa ate some of the Comanche people. I mean, how would you feel if someone ate one of your friends or, worse yet, someone from your family?"

The thought piqued her interest because she had heard of things like eating another human occurring in deepest Peru or darkest Africa but certainly not in America. "I believe you are creating falsehoods to try to frighten me," she burst out. "I shan't have any of it, Mr. O'Cleary!"

He shook his head. "It's the unabated truth, Margaret." Her name just fell out of his mouth. He waited to see if she would correct him.

She just shook her head. "What are the odds that we might meet one of these Comanche Indians while we are traveling?"

"Well, Margaret Mae, somehow I just didn't envision you a gambling gal." He laughed deeply and took the saddle off her mule. "The odds are nil. The US Army has them quite corralled.

There are marshes and swamps that we should worry more about, with the cottonmouths and coral snakes and an occasional copperhead. I want you to pay keen attention where you walk and what's swimming near you when we ford."

Her eyes were wide and glassy.

"I heard that even gators sometimes come this far down."

She stiffened. "Alligators?"

"Yup."

"We surely can't sleep on the ground. Do we make our beds in the trees? I saw the low trees we passed not too long ago." Her brow wrinkled with worry, which was a new sight.

"Nope. We sleep on the ground, rolled up in our..." He paused, remembering how she'd chastised him about buying her that comfortable soogan. She was going to appreciate it when she placed it in her bedroll and she was all cozy for the night. He stopped talking and watched her face.

"I may somehow arrange to sleep in a tree," she announced with some finality.

"Some snakes climb trees. In fact, most can. You might not find that suitable." He grinned.

A gunshot cracked in the air, and then Finn heard Patch yelling, "Injuns! Injuns!" He came galloping madly down the trail on his horse, his legs flying in the air. "Not far! They'll be here soon." He was out of breath but hurriedly dismounted and helped gather their belongings to place them back on the horses and mules.

Finn glanced around their location, his thoughts racing. *There are the bluffs, but they will take too long to climb. The best bet is to get on that low hill, take the high ground, and hope we won't be seen.* He grabbed Margaret's wrist. "Come on!" He yanked her up the hill as Patch gathered the reins of their horses and mules and followed Finn. Once the animals were hidden behind the knoll, Finn whispered, "Which tribe?" hoping it was the Penateka or the Caddo.

Patch whispered back the dreaded answer, "About six renegade Comanche."

Both men glanced at Margaret Mae. Her honey-brown ringlets were matted around her pink cheeks, and her tasseled curls dangled loosely across her back. She was breathing heavily, and her pupils dilated with fear. Both men nodded at the same time.

Margaret saw it. "What?" she whispered, but neither man answered.

Finn knew that if the Comanche overran them, one of them would kill Margaret Mae Ditmar quickly before the Indians had a chance to capture her. Their nod had been a silent affirmation.

Finn's Colt .44 was pointed down the hill. He was grateful they didn't have to watch the bluff behind them. No one could sneak up on them that way. It was a sheer cliff. It was almost dark, and he was having trouble seeing in the twilight. Shadows lurked, and the wind spooked them with noises of birds in the trees or mice scampering along the ground. The three of them lay on their stomachs on top of the hill, watching the trail below.

Hours went by. The moon came up, a half moon that gave them a better view of the trail down below. An owl hooted. Patch nudged Finn with his elbow. They both slid over closer to Margaret, wedging her body between them.

She had perched her chin on her arm, and she too was staring down at the trail. "Are we going to die?" she whispered. Finn wrapped his arm over her back but didn't say a word. She didn't shake his arm off.

They waited...

# CHAPTER SEVEN

The sun came up over the hill, the glow of it burning their eyes and warming them after the long night. Neither man had slept, but Margaret Mae sighed peacefully in her slumber between them. Finn flexed his fingers out and back into a fist several times. He had kept his hand on the butt of his gun all night long. The two men rubbed their eyes and surveyed the clearing down below.

There was no sign of the renegade Comanches.

"I tell you, Finn, I saw them headed this way. Six of 'em."

Margaret opened her eyes. "Is it time for breakfast?" The side of her cheek was marked with small pocks from the tiny stones where she had laid her head through the long night.

"Good morning, Miss Margaret!" Patch inched away from her. "Did you sleep well?"

She sat up and looked around her. "No Indians?"

"Thankfully not." Finn sat up. "We need to scout around to make sure they moved on, but I believe we can safely say that raiding party didn't know we were here."

Patch shook his head. "Comanche know everything, Finn. They knew—they just had better things to tend to. I know one thing. I am glad they moved on. Those are the fiercest warriors and the most brutal. I didn't fancy having my own genitals for breakfast!"

Margaret gasped. "How dare you speak that way and insult me!"

Patch asked, "What? What'd I do?" He shifted onto his knees. "I'm just saying that Comanches are horrid torturers, that's all."

"Need I remind you, Patch, we do have a lady in our presence." Finn said, attempting to apologize for his friend.

Finn helped Margaret to her feet, noticing that her dress was torn and the frock certainly no longer clean and crisp. "That'll be enough of reality talk, Patch." Finn's fingers lightly touched her arm. "He didn't mean to insult you, Miss Ditmar." For some reason, he could feel that she needed to be respected. He removed his fingers immediately from her arm.

She looked into his blue eyes and felt a sincere gratefulness. "Thank you, Mr. O'Cleary."

He thought he saw tears in her eyes and knew he would have no idea what to do with them. He stepped back away from her and looked down the small embankment. "We need to get moving. I want to push to get to Colbert's Crossing into Texas as soon as possible. It's a big push, but I think, givin' what you saw last night, Patch, we shouldn't linger here another second."

Patch nodded. "Six Comanches. They would have made fast killin' of the two of us." He rolled his eyes toward Margaret Mae. "And God knows what they would have done with her." Both men knew exactly what they would have done with the beautiful young woman. At the thought of harm coming to Margaret Mae, Finn once again raised his gun in front of them.

Habitually, he blessed himself with the sign of the cross. "God forbid," he whispered.

Margaret Mae bowed her head when she saw his attempt at prayer. "Dear Lord, thank

You for delivering us from our enemies. We beseech Thee to watch over us this day."

Finn and Patch bowed their heads. The three of them uttered soft *amens* at the end of Margaret Mae's prayer.

They'd started down the hill when suddenly Finn raised his arm in the air. "Stop!"

Patch whispered, "Well, I never."

There at the bottom of the hill, slinking through the tall mesquite grass along the side of the trail, was a gigantic black panther. Its black hide shone in the morning sun, its golden eyes looked straight ahead, and its long tail swished behind. The panther moved swiftly up the trail and in a moment climbed some rocks and was gone.

Patch let out a "Whoo-eee! That thing must've been on its way home after a long night of hunting."

Finn shook his head in disbelief. "I heard that there were black panthers out here, but I just never believed it."

Margaret Mae smiled. "Why, I do believe I now have something to tell my grandchildren one day."

Finn nodded and thought, *She sure has a beautiful smile. I like that about her.* And almost immediately, he thought, *There ain't much to like about Margaret Mae Ditmar, but a smile that sunny has to be appreciated.*

The long days on the trail rolled into long dark nights that were haunted by the screams of mountain lions, coyotes, and bobcats. The little trio didn't see any more Comanches, which made each of them breathe a bit easier. Finn helped Margaret hang her blankets as makeshift walls each night if she found a tree sturdy enough; otherwise, he made sure that she put her bedroll by the fire. He also made sure that he and Patch were sleeping far from where she slept. At first they teased her, but then they began to respect her privacy. Finn and Patch took turns guarding the camp each night in two-hour increments. Often, Finn would find himself staring at Margaret's sleeping face by the embers of the fire.

As he watched her one evening, he thought, *She looks just like an angel when she's sleeping, a darlin' angel, but one would never see her that way in the daylight.* He chuckled aloud softly.

Patch grabbed his friend's arm and shook it, taking Finn away from his moment of reverie. Patch whispered, "Finn, I've been thinking. Maybe I should go ahead of you. I will take my horse and check the trail out a ways. I don't think we can be too careful." Patch had always been a wild one, but he was also a cautious one when he was on the trail. He had seen too much in the past ten years to warrant a total abandonment of caution.

"I'm sure everything's okay, Patch. It's been quiet every night. No one's following us. We double-backed and checked. I believe we are safe. There's just no need."

Patch shook his head. "I heard the hoots and whistles. Those weren't owls and birds."

Finn knew Patch was right. "Okay. I'll give you a half hour out there, but then we are going to follow you if you don't report back. I'm not waitin' here, Patch."

Margaret stretched her arms in the air.

Finn asked her, "Did you sleep well?"

"Of course!" She stretched again.

Patch nodded. "Okay, Finn, half-hour lead time will be just enough time for this little lady to comb those tangled chestnut mornin' curls." He laughed as Margaret Mae's hand immediately went up to her head, trying to adjust her tangled locks.

Finn tried to hand Patch his Colt. "Take my gun, Patch."

Patch answered apologetically, "Ah, no thanks, Finn. You know I have my rope and my blade." He patted his side. "Can't imagine needing a gun. Remember, when you were taggin' behind me, just knee high, I was shootin' a fifty-cent Osage orange-tree bow with sinew string from the butcher when we were boys. I'm not into those guns." He chuckled. "Too dangerous. I might shoot off my own foot."

Finn nodded. "I looked up to you, Patch. You taught me how to use one of those Osage orange-tree bows. We shot a lot of rabbits in those days. You were one good teacher." He had been of the same mind as Patch before he picked up that Colt .44 lying in the dust on Sedalia's dusty road. He lowered the barrel. "We'll wait exactly one half hour, Patch, and then we're comin' after you."

"Why is he going?" Margaret asked. "Do you think it wise for him to go alone? Patch, I don't think you should go alone. The three of us need to stick together."

"Now, Margaret dear, you've touched my heart that you care about the hair on my head, but you see"—he lifted his cowboy hat—"there just tain't no hair here to worry over." His grin made her smile. "I will be back before you can untangle that mass of knots on yer head."

Patch nodded and then continued down the mountain, guiding his horse behind him. When he got to the bottom of the rise, he mounted.

He didn't look back at them but swung his leg over his horse as he took off down the trail. Finn watched until he couldn't see the horse any more.

"Will he be all right?" Margaret was combing her curls, just as Patch had said. She twisted each honey-brown curl around her finger, and amazingly, each one stayed coiled. Then, she pulled them all back and knotted them at the nape of her neck.

"Miss Margaret, I have some beef jerky if you are hungry. We won't be fixin' breakfast this morning." Finn went to his saddlebag and drew out the dried beef.

For once, she didn't protest when he handed it to her. "Thank you. I am worried about Patch. You're sure he will be all right?" She sounded genuinely concerned.

"Patch can take care of himself." He gave her the canteen. "Hope you won't mind that I drank off it. It's a new wood one, though," he said apologetically.

She paused a moment, looked into his clear blue eyes, and took the canteen. She gulped the water. When she stopped and pulled it away from her lips, a dribble of the clear, warm liquid ran down her chin. She handed the canteen to him.

"Had enough?" he asked.

She nodded.

He pressed his lips to the spout and drank two swallows, and he could smell her scent on the canteen, that delightful lingering vanilla scent. For a moment, he thought of her soft pink lips on the edges of the spout, the same spout where his lips were pressing tightly. *What a curious thought.* He wondered why it had come into his head.

His eyes watched her face as he drank. *Why, Miss Margaret Mae Ditmar is quite pretty when she wakes up in the morning and hasn't started to speak much.* He almost laughed but thought better of it. He wanted more water, but there wasn't much chance they would find decent water until they reached Colbert's Ferry Crossing, and he wanted to be sure he had enough for her. He could always drink the whiskey he had in his saddlebag.

"Do you believe we will find more dangerous Indians on the trail?" Her voice was a bit unsteady. This frightened and unsteady woman was definitely not the Margaret Mae he had come to know in his brief encounters with her on the trail.

"Don't you worry, Miss Ditmar. Patch and I can keep you safe. You will not experience any dread while we are by your side–not one moment." He remembered the silent pact he and Patch had made about her safety. He felt a strange groundswell travel through his body, which made his stomach seem to knot and release. He certainly was not accustomed to that type of undulation.

A half hour had passed. Patch did not return. Finn snatched at the reins of his horse and the two mules. "Come on, Miss Ditmar. We have to get going now." He felt a moment of trepidation. One thing Patch was guaranteed to be was punctual. *This is definitely not like him*, he thought.

Margaret Mae followed behind the two mules down the hill. Once at the bottom, after kicking her foot several times into a tear on her skirt, she asked, "May I borrow your knife, Mr. O'Cleary?"

Finn looked at her. "What do you plan to do with my knife? Miss Ditmar, it is quite sharp."

"Hopefully so. I plan to cut off the hem of my dress."

He did not say I *told you* so but silently handed the knife to her and watched as she sat on a stump and took off nearly eight inches from the bottom of her gown. Then she cut through her white lace petticoat, taking it off right at the top of her square-toed black boots. Finn was fascinated that the boot's toe was decorated with light-blue flowers.

Her eyes caught him looking. "The least you could do, Mr. O'Cleary, is look away." He thought he saw a slight smile on her soft pink lips. "I suppose the damage is done."

"I didn't mean to be disrespectful."

She waved the blade of the knife at him as she spoke. "Looking at a lady's ankles could be taken quite seriously as a breach of proper conduct, Mr. O'Cleary. I am sure my father would certainly object."

He knew that was not an idle threat. Her father would indeed object, he was sure. He turned his back to her to let her complete her task. "Honest, Margaret Mae, I meant no disrespect."

She didn't answer him.

*Oh dread, and now she's angry with me again. How long will it be this time?*

Then, like a crack of thunder, she screamed.

He turned quickly and witnessed a snake with bright-orange and black rings dangling from her outstretched hand. He ran toward her as the snake dropped off and slithered rapidly away down a burrow.

She began to cry, considerable enormous tears zigzagging down her cheeks. Finn reached into his vest pocket, but he promptly brought out his empty hand. There was no handkerchief to wipe her face, so he placed his hands on her cheeks, trying to hold back her tears. He softly patted away the salty droplets. He whispered, "No, no, Maggie, don't cry. Please don't cry. You're going to be okay. Don't cry."

She sobbed even more shrilly as she held her hand with her other hand. "It's a coral snake, Finn. A deadly envenomation is going to take my life before I can see my father!" She sobbed so loudly that birds flew away from the trees overhead. "I'm going to die, Finn!" she wailed.

Finn lifted her up and then sat down on the stump with her held firmly on his lap. He began rocking her back and forth, as if she was a baby or a small child. "No, no, Maggie, listen to me. You are going to be fine. I saw the snake, and—"

She buried her face in his neck and held tightly to his shirt, her entire body convulsing with her sobs. Her tears soaked his shirt.

"Please, stop crying, Maggie, so you can hear me."

She choked back a sob and then began to cry again. "But, Finn, it was a deadly coral snake. I am going to succumb to neuromuscular–"

He pushed her away from him and took her slender shoulders in his large, strong hands. He squeezed tightly. "You are not going to die. Are you listening? You are going to be okay. Can you hear me now?"

Her sob caught in her throat, and she looked into his calm cerulean eyes. She stopped crying. "But–"

"Listen, dearest. Yes, the snake indeed looked like a coral snake, but it was a red-on-black snake. There was no venom. None." He lifted her hand to take a look at the bite. "You undoubtedly sat on his hiding place." On her red swelling skin, where the snake had bit her hand, were two indentions. "Let's pour some whiskey on this bite, and then we have to get going." He lifted her up and stood her on her feet.

"I'm not going to die?"

He grinned. "Not today, my dear Miss Maggie."

"Quit calling me Maggie!" She held her bitten hand gingerly with her other hand. Her eyes were red and swollen.

"I kind of like saying it. Maggie. Maggie. Maggie Ditmar. Yup. Nice ring to it. Maggie it is!" He chuckled and reached for his saddlebag to draw out the whiskey flask. "I hate to waste good whiskey, but I know a little on those puncture holes there will do you good, and maybe you should have a swig to calm your nerves."

He poured a small amount over the snakebite. Her eyes filled with tears when she felt the sting of the alcohol on the open wound. He said, "Now, take a sip."

She turned her face away.

"Now go on, do it!" he ordered.

She took a sip, and her whole face seemed to pucker and draw up into her lips.

He laughed. "It's amazing to me what some gals will do to get a sip of whiskey. I tell you, Maggie Ditmar, you are one remarkable gal."

He looked at the uneven rim of her dyed mauve dress, poised at the top of her tiny black square-tipped boots with the tiny flowers. Her honey-brown tresses, released from the confines of her bonnet, were dangling against her back.

"And you, sir, are one vile despicable vagabond." She turned from him as she mounted her mule. "Come, Annabelle, let's put some distance between this disgusting example of a man and us."

"Annabelle?" Finn cocked his head to one side. "You named your mule?"

"I named both of them, Annabelle and Lizzy." She gently kicked Annabelle's sides, and the mule obliged by moving forward down the trail. She turned and called over her shoulder, "Mister O'Cleary, shouldn't we be moving a little faster to find your friend?"

Finn swung his body into the saddle as he shook his head. *Darn woman! I'm not ready to throw up the sponge and let her win! This is war, but darn, she is dreadfully pretty!* He hated himself for even thinking it. The trail ahead was long and dangerous. He had no room in his head for thoughts about a pretty woman. He began to imagine Maggie with warts on the end of her nose, but he still saw her cocoa-brown eyes and her pouty pink mouth.

# CHAPTER EIGHT

Finn saw the horse first. It was leisurely munching on grass alongside the trail, its reins hanging loose across the saddle—Patch's saddle.

Maggie pulled up her reins when she saw the horse. "Where's Patch?" Her voice cracked slightly as she slid from her mule. "Where is he, Finn?"

"Take cover over by that rock, Maggie. And for God's sake, keep your mouth quiet!" He watched as Maggie ran for the rock and hid behind it. He slowly went up to the horse and grabbed its reins. He took his Colt out of its holster and walked steadily forward. His eyes scanned the horizon, and then he looked around the area near him.

Patch was lying across the narrow trail, his lariat trailing from one hand and stretching past his head disappearing in the tall grass.

Finn knelt next to him. "Patch! Patch!" He saw an arrow stuck in his friend's chest and immediately noticed that the arrow went through Patch's shoulder and was stuck deep into the ground, pinning Patch to the dirt. Finn put his hand on Patch's chest. "You're okay, Patch. I'm gonna fix you up as good as new."

Patch's eyes watered, and he whispered, "Six of 'em, jus' like I said, Finn. They killed all the others. All ten." He wet his lips with his tongue. "Scalped them all. Somethin' spooked them, or they would have scalped me too." Any other time, Finn would have reminded Patch that he didn't have any hair, but the humor was lost when he stared down at the pool of black surrounding Patch.

"Quiet now, Patch. I gotta get you fixed up. I'm going to get Maggie, and then we can move you to a safer spot."

Patch tried to laugh. "I'm not going anywhere, Finn."

Finn hurried back to the spot where he had told Maggie to hide. "Come on Maggie. Patch's been hit. He has an arrow clear through his shoulder. We gotta get him to safety and fix him up." He glanced at her shortened skirt. "Did you save that material you cut off?"

She nodded. "In my saddlebag."

"Good. We'll use it for bandages. Come on. He's lost a lot of blood, but I think he is going to be okay."

She hesitated.

"This is *no* time to become a docile little lady, Margaret Mae Ditmar!"

As if he had poked her with a red-hot iron, she ran quickly to her saddlebag and retrieved the material. She glanced up at him. "And we'll need your whiskey, Finn, like you used on my hand."

"That's why I brought it. Never know when someone might need a swig."

She glanced at her hand. It had festered slightly, but otherwise, she was fine. She knelt next to Patch, visibly controlling herself when she saw the arrow sticking out of his shoulder and pinning him to the ground. She put her hand on his forehead. "You are going to be all right now, Patch. We're here with you."

His eyes fluttered open, and he smiled. "Why, lookie here. My own angel of death, and such a pretty little angel at that. How'd I get so darn lucky?"

She raised her voice. "Quit talking like that, Patch!" She looked at Finn. "Can we take the arrow out, Finn?"

Finn shook his head. "Not yet. I want to make a fire so that we can cauterize the wound closed. Wish we had a fire pot. At least if we had one of those fire pots filled with coals hanging on the back of a wagon, we wouldn't have to start a fire from scratch. Now it's going take a while." He turned toward Patch. "Patch, I am going to lift you to a safer spot. It's going to feel somethin' terrible but has to be done. Can't leave you lying out here, exposed on the trail. We're near the bluffs now, and we have to climb up there to have a safe perch."

Patch whispered, "You do what you have to do, friend. Jus' give me some bark to bite on so I won't make noise and summon those dread Comanches back to finish me off and take a whack at you and Maggie!"

Finn placed a thick twig in Patch's mouth and pulled his friend up off the ground into his arms. The arrow popped out of the ground, and then the bloody tip of it was exposed, for the shaft was still imbedded through Patch's shoulder. Finn carried his friend's heavy body to a thicket of trees not far off the trail.

Maggie followed closely behind. She had the reins of all the animals clutched in her tiny hands and had to yank fiercely on them to make all of the animals close ranks, bumping their bodies together to follow her.

Finn immediately began to make a fire using dry, loose twigs. "As soon as I get this fire going, we can use the hot twigs, and then I can take the arrow out." He glanced down at Patch's sleeping face. "I hope he stays out." He handed the wooden canteen to Maggie. "Put a little water on his lips every now and again."

"Finn, won't the fire attract the Comanches?"

"Have to chance it. I need to seal him up so he won't get an infection."

Once Finn felt he had done everything he could to help his friend, he was able to turn to the task of burying the rest of his friends. First, he glanced at Maggie. She was sitting on a blanket with Patch's head in her lap. His shoulder was neatly patched with the scraps from Maggie's dress. Her hand combed Patch's hair over and over. She ran her fingers through it and hummed. The wound had been washed with the whiskey, and a hot poker had sealed it. Patch slept. "He will sleep a while now, Maggie. If you don't mind staying with him, I have to go bury my friends."

Maggie shook her head. "Finn, you don't even have a shovel."

Finn raised his hands in the air, their backs to her. "The good Lord gave me these before he gave me a shovel. It will be a while. Here." He handed her his Colt. "If Indians come back, Maggie, shoot Patch and then shoot yourself. Can you do that, Maggie?"

She was stunned silent.

"Can you?" he asked again, urgently.

She nodded.

"Tell me. Tell me you will do it, Maggie."

Her big brown eyes became even larger. "I can do it, Finn. I've heard the horrible stories. I know the reason why you are asking."

"Say you *will* do it."

"I will do it."

He looked into her eyes, wanting to reach out and hug her and know that she was safe, but instead, he just said, "Good."

Satisfied that she would follow his directions, he turned and walked toward the meadow where the ten cowboys were lying with arrows shot into various parts of their bodies. Just as Patch had said, each one was scalped clean, and from what Finn could tell, several of them had been alive when it was done. He knelt down and began to dig. Tears streaked down his cheeks.

*Sometimes, being a man is knowing when to cry.*

# CHAPTER NINE

Dawn crept up before he finished sliding each cold, stiff body into its grave. The graves were shamefully shallow, but he had put as many rocks as he could find atop them, hoping the coyotes and other wild animals wouldn't dig them up. Each grave had a makeshift cross of wood. He had taken his knife and carved each of their names: Douglas, Samuel, Everett, Ollie, Horace, Bundy, Tip, Jeremy, Faust, and Kritz.

He ran his fingers through his hair. "Christ, it would have been Patch and I here, too, if we hadn't picked up Miss Ditmar." He shook his head. "How in the heck am I going to tell their folks?" He had known most of them since he was a boy. He fell on his knees. "Lord, please receive them with your open arms." He touched the cross that Bundy had worn. "He was such a good chuck-wagon—" He couldn't finish as a lump closed his throat.

He didn't see Maggie standing behind him. She had the Colt in her hand. Its muzzle was facing down. Her voice was lifeless and flat. "Dig another grave, Finn. Patch is gone."

"How? It was just a flesh wound through his shoulder. Can't be! He's sleepin' deep, that's all."

She shook her head. "He convulsed. The arrow must've been poisoned. That's all I can think of." She swayed and then collapsed onto the ground.

He ran to her and pulled her into his arms. They both cried, pulling each other as close as they could. He grabbed her curls in his fists and squeezed them as he pushed her face into his chest. The prairie wind whipped her soft curls up into his face. As he rocked her gently in his arms, he saw the ten crosses standing sentinel across the meadow. He couldn't speak, couldn't cry another tear. He just watched the grass blowing like gentle waves upon a golden sea.

They stayed like that, holding each other there on the prairie, oblivious to any dangers that might be lurking, just finding solace in the arms of the living amidst the resting place of the departed.

Finn began to dig Patch's grave. He didn't speak but just kept dragging his hands through the red earth over and over again. Maggie began to dig, too. She dragged her small hands through the dirt. Finn was faster and dug deeper and more quickly than she, but they both kept digging. The sun beat on their backs, and they just kept at it. Their clothes were drenched with sweat, but they kept digging.

Finn whispered, "I want Patch to lie deep and safe." Maggie nodded her head silently in agreement. Finally, Finn jumped into the hole and began to toss the dirt and rocks out. Finn kept digging. Maggie noticed that his hands were bleeding. When the grave came up to his waist, he nodded to her. Patch's final resting place was ready.

She cried softly as Finn pushed the freshly dug earth over Patch's body. Then, when it was done, when she could no longer see Patch's face, she bowed her head and began the prayer she had memorized when she was three years old. "The Lord is my shepherd. I shall not want. He maketh me to lie down in green pastures. He leadeth me beside the still waters. He restoreth my soul. He leadeth me in the paths of righteousness for his name's sake.

Yea, though I walk through the valley of the shadow of death, I will fear no evil, for thou art with me. Thy rod and thy staff, they comfort me. Thou preparest a table before me in the presence of mine enemies. Thou anointest my head with oil. My cup runneth over. Surely, goodness and mercy shall follow me all the days of my life, and I will dwell in the house of the Lord forever."

Finn reached his hand down, took Maggie's hand in his, and said, "Our Father, which art in Heaven, hallowed be thy name. Thy kingdom come. Thy will be done in earth as it is in Heaven. Give us, this day, our daily bread and forgive us our trespasses as we forgive them that trespass against us. And lead us not into temptation but deliver us from evil, for thine is the kingdom, the power, and the glory for ever and ever." He paused and squeezed Maggie's hand. They both looked at the small field of crosses and said in unison, "Amen."

# CHAPTER TEN

Maggie took the pannier off Annabelle and dropped it and most of its contents on the side of the trail. She knew she wouldn't be wearing those fancy dresses and wire-framed bonnets anymore. She kept the books she had tied to her saddle—Longfellow's *Hiawatha*, Thoreau's *Walden*, and Whitman's *Leaves of Grass*—even though Harriet Beecher Stowe's School for Women had been a lifetime ago. She stood very still, watching the waves rolling across the blades of grass in the meadow, interrupted only by the freshly made graves. Her eyes became glassy, but she didn't cry anymore.

She placed her foot in the stirrup and plopped down atop Annabelle. Finn had the reins of Lizzy and Patch's horse. They started down the trail, headed for the Red River crossing. Finn was quiet, like a ghost rider on his horse. He didn't look at her but just stared straight ahead, keeping his horse tight on the trail. She turned her head to keep her eyes on Patch's grave for as long as she could. Then finally, he was out of sight, and she had to turn around in her saddle. Her heart ached so badly that she expected her body to open up and let all the backed-up blood flow out, but of course, it would not.

An occasional turkey or deer darted across their path, but for the most part, they just kept moving forward. At one point, he drew up his horse's reins and stopped. He pointed at a thicket of blackberries and waited while she gathered some in her skirt.

She carried them to him. "Have some." She smiled, but her smile did not light up her eyes.

He shook his head.

She ripped a square of her skirt, sealed the berries into it, and climbed back onto Annabelle, and they continued on their way.

By the time evening approached, Maggie was riding Annabelle right next to Finn's horse. She finally spoke to him, "So why didn't we go down the river by riverboat?"

He didn't look at her. "There is no riverboat. There's what they call the Great Raft, caused by jammed logs blocking the river. It's even called the Great Raft 'cause nothin' can move. There's no sailing past it. Only way across the Red River is by barge at Colbert's Crossing at Red River Station. Colbert's an Indian. He runs the barge. Sometimes, there's a long line waiting to cross, especially with the longhorns needing passage. But with the steer fever, there won't be any longhorns." He finally turned toward her. "Let's stop, and you can have some water, and I'll try to get us some supper." He slid off his horse.

She climbed off Annabelle then reached out and pulled on his elbow. "Finn, I'm truly sorry about your friend, Patch."

He paused a moment to look into her eyes. "Seems he was your friend, too, Maggie."

She nodded. "But I know he was yours for a long time. I don't have long-time friends like that. Can't imagine what losing someone so close... Well, my mother, of course, but other than her..." She stopped speaking.

He looked up at the sky. "It's going to pour buckets soon. End-of-summer rains are no picnic. Let's make camp under that ridge there, and I will get us some supper. Maybe I can lasso one of those ground-walking turkeys."

The smile was his first since he had buried his friends. His face was so tanned that his white teeth seemed to glow. "We can head for Colbert's Crossing in the morning."

Her voice was unsteady. "Will the Comanches come back?"

He shook his head thoughtfully. "By now, they have moved on. I doubt if they would come anywhere near the crossing. Too many folks there with guns." He put his hand on hers, still at his elbow. "Try not to worry, Maggie." He patted her hand. "I will get you to your father. I always keep my promises. No harm's going to come to you."

He dropped his hand and walked his horse to the ridge. It would protect them if it did rain, she could see that, but she wondered what sort of animals might be lurking in that small cave-like opening. As if in answer to her question, a small black bear came snorting toward Finn. It almost caught him by surprise with its gigantic black paw thudding against his chest, pushing him to the ground as it ran toward the tall grass. He drew his gun to shoot and then lowered the barrel. "He won't bother us anymore." He stood back up. "I believe that was a close one!" He put his hand to his chest. The bear's claw had ripped through the leather of his vest.

"Are you sure the bear won't come back even if we have stolen his home?" she asked.

"I don't think he lives here. He's a young one just out scouting for his winter hibernation place. We'll be fine." He dropped his saddlebag onto the dirt. "We can tie the animals close in here, where they will be safe from predators tonight, and we can bunk under this rock." He slapped the top of the entrance. He didn't speak again but handed her his gun and then headed out toward the flats with his rope and knife at the ready to find something for supper.

Maggie watched Finn leave and then spread out her bedroll and sat on it. She pulled her knees up to her chin, placed the Colt .44 on her knees, and waited. Her eyes steadily watched out the opening of the cavern. She was keenly aware of any movement in the tall grass. She watched as a hawk soared down and fell into the grass and then flew back up with a mouse in its talons. She heard a rustle and looked up and saw that the ceiling of the small cavern was lined with bats.

She caught her breath. "Oh my, I hope you all stay put on that ceiling!" The undisturbed bats did just that. She watched them for a time but finally trusted that they weren't going to charge at her head.

Shadows appeared as the sun began to fade from the sky. Fear gently gripped her stomach. *What if Finn doesn't come back?* She brushed the thought aside. She crawled out the opening and began to gather wood. "Make yourself useful, Margaret Mae Ditmar," she said aloud. Then, as an afterthought, she said, "Get a move on, Maggie." She didn't stop until her arms were loaded with branches and twigs. She dropped them at the mouth of the cavern. Then, she headed out again to get another armful. She didn't see the silhouette coming toward the camp. She had left the gun lying on the bedroll.

By the time the silhouette got close enough for her to recognize it, Finn was yelling at her, "Why did you leave the cavern? Didn't I tell you to stay in there? What if a wolf or a mountain lion were to come—or worse yet, the Comanche came back?" As Finn screamed, he adjusted a deer on his shoulders and then threw the dead creature onto the ground.

She shook her head. "I thought I should gather wood to make a fire. I—"

"You thought? You thought! Did you think about cougars and panthers and Indians?" he continued screaming. "If you were a sister of mine, I would turn you over my knee and whoop you with one of those twigs you've gathered—that's exactly what I would do!"

Tears formed in her eyes. At that point in his life, her tears were the one thing Finn feared most in the whole world.

"No, now don't you cry! Stop that now!" He was still yelling until he saw furrows of mud beginning to run down her cheeks. "Now, ah, Maggie, I'm sorry. Please stop crying. I jus' can't take it. I just don't want to lose anyone else I care about. That's all. Don't cry." He reached out to grab her, but she bumped into his side and went into the cavern. She put her face into the bedroll to smother her sobs, but he heard them just the same.

*Darn women! Why hadn't my da warned me about these most frustrating, perplexing, annoying, whimpering, sauce-box creatures? I learned about bows and arrows and knives and guns—how to skin a deer, how to cook a good campfire stew, how not to drink strange water, but Da never told me one single thing about a woman. Why, their tears are worse than a Red River flood—or even worse than that! They are just downright...* His thoughts stopped as he watched her body shaking with her sobs. He couldn't take another moment of watching her cry.

He turned his back, walked to a nearby tree, and swung the small deer up to hook it on a broken branch. He quickly cut out the anus and around the deer's colon. He nipped through the fat, careful not to cut through the intestines. He took both his hands and spread the deer's pelvis until it cracked. Then, he ran his knife up to its ribcage. He cut all the entrails away, freeing the guts, and then he pulled them out of the body. The excess blood drained out of the deer's body onto the dirt. The appearance of blood unnerved him for a moment as a flash of Patch's body, lying in the wet black earth, shot through his memory.

He stood back and looked at the deer. "Nice," he whispered softly. He grabbed all the entrails and fat, walked to the edge of the river, and tossed them in. He watched to see if any gators came to claim the prize, but none did. "Oh, you're going to come, but I don't have time to watch." He strolled back to the camp and glanced at the cavern's opening. Maggie was lying quietly on her stomach. He couldn't tell whether she was asleep or not.

He made the fire and sliced most of the venison off the deer's bones. The pieces for their dinner that night were thicker, but the rest he sliced thin. He skewered the meat on posts and put it over the fire.

The smoke curled into the evening sky. The stars had begun to pop out. The half moon inched its way up. The treeline had become a blur in the dark.

He ventured, "Ah, come on, Maggie. The stars are coming out. The deer's going to be cooked soon." He turned and saw her watching him, her knees pulled up under her chin and her face resting on her hands poised on her knees. Her golden-brown curls were fluffed all over her head. "Maggie, I'm sorry," he whispered.

She smiled. "I can't hear you, Finn O'Cleary. What's that you said?"

He raised his voice. "I said that I am sorry, Margaret Mae Ditmar."

She nodded. "That's what I thought you said. I forgive you."

He turned the green branches spearing the meat, checking which pieces of venison were ready. "Come here, Maggie. Time to get some food in that growling stomach of yours. I could hear it growling clear out here. I thought the black bear had come back." He grinned.

She scrambled out from the opening of the cavern. "I thought you'd never ask." She took the branch from his hand, the venison skewered on the end. She waited for it to cool a bit and then took a big bite. "Oh, Finn, it's wonderful!"

He winked at her. "I knew you'd like it, Miss Margaret Mae Ditmar." For the first time ever, she saw the dimples appear in his bronzed cheeks.

The next long days went by without incident. Margaret rolled out her bedroll close to the fire each night. Finn slept on the other side of the fire, his Colt at the ready. His sleep was shallow, most of the time with one eye open. Maggie slept as if she was a baby safe in its cradle...

# CHAPTER ELEVEN

Finn watched each morning as Maggie rolled up her bedroll and meticulously tied the ends. She ran a tortoise comb through her hair, parting it down the middle, and then she piled it all on the back of her head in a roll, securing it tightly in a bun before putting on her tattered and torn bonnet. She tied both sets of ribbons under her chin instead of the usual one bow. He smiled at her determination to keep the bonnet in place.

Another uneventful night passed, his sleep edgy and agitated. He kept remembering the details of the last days, especially the loss of his childhood friend. He ran the memories through his mind—how he wished with all his heart that things could have gone differently *if* he hadn't sent Patch out there alone, *if* they had left later or earlier, or *if* they had gone with the others and not brought Miss Margaret Mae Ditmar with them. No matter how he considered the events, they always had the same ending. Patch O'Riley was gone, and Finn knew he wouldn't see him again in this world. The other reality that kept him from falling into a deep sleep was that the Comanche were on the move, and he had to keep that young woman safe until he could deliver her to the arms of her father. No way was he going to allow himself to doze deeply and be ambushed by crazed Indians!

The small fire had smoked all night. Maggie poked at it with a long stick then turned and looked at him. "I sure will be exultant when we can have an egg or some porridge." She wrinkled her nose and put her hands on her hips. "In Connecticut, we had poached eggs, thick bacon, and toast every morning." Her eyes had a dreamy, faraway look. "We sat down at white linen tablecloths with real polished silver forks and knives."

"Did you now?" His hand brushed through his hair. "At dear Miss Beecher's School, I presume?"

"Of course. It was quite refined, you know. Every woman there was utterly polished and sophisticated." She brushed one of her ringlets from her eye. "The school is absolutely distinguished." She tilted her head back slightly.

"I'm sure." He couldn't help the grin that overtook his face. "Your extremely wise father had hoped that you would become a gracious, cultivated young woman."

"What are you saying? Are you saying that I have not?"

"I'm not saying anything."

"You are! Finn O'Cleary, you are saying that I am not gracious and cultivated. That's what you are saying!" She raised her voice and folded her arms in front of her.

"I'm not saying that, Maggie."

"Don't call me Maggie! You are implying, sir, that I am neither gracious nor cultivated. Do not let my appearances fool you." She reached down, pulled up her tattered dress, and then released it again. "I stand to remind you that when you first met me, I was dressed in the most unsurpassed Paris finery one could purchase in Hartford." She looked down at her gown, torn and blotched with red dirt and the blood of Patch O'Riley. When she saw the blood on her gown, she turned toward the fire, putting her back to Finn. "I have no desire to argue with you early in the morning, Finn O'Cleary."

"Good. Let's eat and get moving. I want us to keep pushin' toward Colbert's Crossing. It's a trek and a push." He reached out and grasped her arm, turning her toward him. "We can buy corn after crossing the river so that you can have some porridge." His voice was soft and apologetic. "There will be plenty of fish to eat, like blue catfish and perch. You can even get some soap." He looked into her eyes. "Give me your hands."

She held out one hand.

"No, both your hands, and hold them close together."

She put her hands palms up, close together.

He placed something smooth and round in her palms. "But for now, these will have to do."

"Turtle eggs! Oh, Finn!" She squealed with delight. "Wherever did you get them?"

"I picked the pocket of a turtle." He grinned. "Isn't that what we vagabonds do?"

She looked down as he reminded her of her temper tantrum when he said the word *vagabond*. "Thank you. They're absolutely perfect."

"We have to hurry, so put them in the fire to start cooking. There will undoubtedly be lines of people waiting to get across at Colbert's. We have to push for a couple of days. We need to get in that line."

Her eyes lit up. "Oh, Finn, perhaps I could find a place to have a bath?"

He loved when her smile lit up her chocolate eyes. "Well, Dennison is only four miles from the crossing, and there might be a nice family that would take us in and let you use their washtub."

Margaret swung herself in a circle. "Oh, that would be absolutely brilliant! I would love it more than having a bite of Mr. Ghirardelli's chocolate!"

Finn began to laugh. "That much? I was thinking of buying some of Mr. Ghirardelli's chocolate for you once we got to a town, but since acquiring a tub and water is so much easier and much cheaper than chocolates, I will reconsider!" His laughter echoed in the trees.

She paid him no heed as she rolled the turtle eggs onto a stone on the edge of the fire. *It's going to be a good day, and nothing Finn O'Cleary says today or does today is going to make me change my mind!*

Most days, they rode in silence. Their mouths were dry, their lips parched. Maggie draped her ribbons over her mouth to keep out the dirt, but she still felt grit between her teeth. Each day tumbled into the next. The red dirt caked on their faces, and the red mud ran down their sweating necks. They averaged about fifteen to twenty miles a day.

When Finn announced, "There it is! I see Colbert's Crossing!" she almost lost her foothold in the stirrups in her excitement and much-needed relief.

As predicted, a long line of wagons and people was waiting to cross at Colbert's Crossing—on both sides of the river. When they saw the line, it became quite evident to the two weary travelers that they wouldn't be crossing very soon. Finn and Maggie might have to wait days or even weeks before it would be their turn to cross. The Indian, Colbert, moved the barge across the river as quickly as he could, but only one wagon could be put on the barge at a time, and if it had two teams of horses, transport took even longer. Colbert's mules pulled the rope, and the barge moved slowly across the Red River.

Maggie put her hands on her hips. "I could swim 'cross this river faster than that barge."

Finn grinned. "I'm sure you could if the current wasn't so swift. And the river is really deep here, Maggie."

"I'll bet Annabelle could swim me 'cross faster than that barge."

Finn nodded. "I have to agree with you, but then we would find you dead, floating faceup somewhere downriver. Better swimmers and stronger men than you have tried."

"But Annabelle could do it, couldn't she Finn? She's so strong." She ran her hand over Annabelle's neck. She had grown quite fond of the mule.

"Perhaps, but I don't suggest you try it."

"But we are so close! I can already feel my father's arms around me! I can't believe how far we've come. Why, to think just days ago I was sitting propped up on the porch of the hotel, waiting for my Annabelle to be delivered so that I could ride to Texas."

Finn nodded. "Just days ago, Patch and I were laughing together." A cloud of pain filled his face at the mention of his friend.

They both stopped talking and watched the other travelers mingling with each other. Some of them had been there for quite some time. The small camp near the water's edge was teeming with people from all over the world. Soldiers were headed for Wyoming and Montana, and leftover gold-rush miners were headed to Oregon or California or Idaho. German families, Irish families, Mexican families, and even a sprinkling of British families were all in line, waiting.

"Where you and your missus headed, mister?" A gentleman dressed in a Texas Ranger's uniform chewed on his tobacco as he spoke to Finn.

"Uh, she... we..." Finn paused and looked at Maggie. *Will she keep her mouth shut if I just go along with him?* he asked himself before he spoke. "We are headed for New Braunfels."

"You don't say? Mostly German folks up in that part. My name's Lawrence Sullivan Ross. Friends call me Sul." He stretched out his arm.

Finn shook his hand. "I'm Finn O'Cleary. From Irish Flats."

"Ah, in truth, I knew your brogue as soon as you opened your mouth." The Ranger grinned. "You and the missus traveling alone?" His eyebrows raised in concern.

"Yep."

"Well, at least you made it safely here. It's about halfway. There's Comanche raiding parties all over the place out there on the prairie. Governor Sam Houston has sent us Rangers out here to keep the peace and keep settlers safe." He was still holding onto Finn's hand as he spoke. He finally released it and let his hand drop to his side.

Finn looked into the ranger's eyes. "We didn't get here unscathed, sir. My group of eleven other men, cattle wranglers, were all massacred by Comanche." He cleared his throat nervously. "We were saved by the good grace of God since we were traveling much slower behind them. I buried all my friends out there." Finn bowed his head. "They didn't have a chance with those Comanches."

"Sorry to hear that, sir. Well, you can understand then why Governor Houston sees fit to send the Rangers out to end these raids by these renegade Indians. There's going to be an eventual eradication of the enemy. I just don't see any other solution."

Finn was standing in front of Maggie. She was listening quietly. She wanted to correct Finn and the ranger and found it quite difficult to keep her mouth shut. She put her hand over her mouth so she wouldn't blurt out that she was indeed *not* Finn O'Cleary's wife, nor would she ever desire to be. She had to admit, though, that he had brought her safely to the Texas border, and she had no doubt he would bravely get her to her father. Of that she was certain.

She came out from behind Finn and spoke to the Ranger. "It was dreadfully frightening out there on the prairie! There were six Comanche, you know."

The Ranger removed his hat and bowed slightly. "Pleased to meet you, Mrs. O'Cleary." She cringed and swallowed. She felt Finn's boot pressing on top of hers. She snapped her head to look into his eyes as she thought, *You need not worry, Finn O'Cleary. I'm not that stupid. My reputation is at stake here. I know when to keep my mouth closed.*

But she couldn't keep her mouth completely closed. Keeping her mouth closed was a feat that Margaret Mae had never quite mastered. "So, Mister Ross, I couldn't help but hear that you are an Indian fighter with the Texas Rangers."

He smiled. "I am that, little lady."

Her eyes narrowed. "I do believe you should kill each and every single Indian you find!"

He shook his head. "Well now, I can understand your disdain for certain Indians, like the Comanches who murdered your friends; however, there are certain Indians that are quite civilized and abiding, like that Indian movin' the barge. He owns it. He paid for it fair and square. And the Tonkawas on the Brazo Reservation, or even the Wacos, who are the Wichita tribe descendants, are decent folks once you get to know them. Why, some of those Indians are Texas Rangers fighting other Indians." He continued to hold his hat in his hand in front of him. "Or then take the Lipan Apache, Chief Castro and Chief Flacco, both are valued allies of the Texas Rangers."

Her body stiffened, and she nodded, hardly knowing how to respond.

Ross put his hat back on his head. "Well, I will bid you adieu, Madame. May you have a safe journey. If there is anything I can do for you two, do not hesitate to call on me."

She watched the Ranger stride away and shook her head vigorously. "He's an Indian lover who kills Indians. This world is definitely not black and white."

"It's a complex world, Mrs. O'Cleary," he teased and waited for her reaction.

"I don't mind keeping up your charade, Finn O'Cleary. It can't be helped to save my reputation. I can't imagine what these kind women here would think of me if they knew I was an unmarried woman accompanied by a man. Well, yes, I do know what they would think!" She looked behind him and saw one of the women headed their way. "Tarnation! Look what's headed this way!"

"Maggie, watch your tongue!" He turned around to see a stout, smiling woman with apple-red cheeks headed their way. She carried a loaf of bread in her outstretched palms and had a huge smile on her face.

"Welcome, neighbors!" The woman's voice was as cheery as her dumpling body was stout. "I saw you come into camp, and I thought, oh my, what they need is a nice loaf of my bread." Her smile squeezed her eyes into slits. "I was telling my friend, Bonnie, that you probably would want a nice, hot bath after the trail, too. You'll like Bonnie, she's a good 'un."

Margaret eyed her with suspicion. *Has this woman been listening to our conversation?* But hearing the word "bath" made her swoon. "Oh, heavens yes. I would love a nice, hot bath."

The woman laughed. "Oh, all us women have the same thought once we get here." She grabbed Margaret's arm. "My name's Ida Drisco. You come with me, and life is going to get much better pretty quickly. I have a big iron tub and water on the fire, right this moment. I may even have a clean gown for you. Might be a bit big, but we can nip and tuck here and there." She reached her fingers out and pinched Margaret's waist when she said the words "here" and "there." "You're a skinny one, that's for sure, but we can work it out. We have plenty of time. We sisters know how to help each other." She hugged Maggie warmly.

Margaret glanced at Finn. He had folded his arms across his chest, and his lips were tilted up slightly in that look he got when he was totally amused. She wanted to spit some good harsh words right at him, but instead she let Ida take her arm. "Nice to meet you, Ida. I'm Margaret Mae." The only thing she kept hearing in her head was the word "bath."

The woman patted her cheek. "You're a sweet one, that's for sure, Margaret Mae. Where you and the mister headed?"

"New Braunfels."

"Lovely place. Me and my man are headed for Irish Flats. We aren't Irish, but we're Catholic, and we heard that there's a great school there for boys. Oh, I do go on! Well, let me tell you, we have plenty of time to get to know each other before the crossing. Me and my family have been here going on six days now. It'll be a while." The woman's arm closed around her shoulders and squeezed. "It is so precious to find such a delightful young woman to forge a friendship with after all these long miles. I have six boys and a girl. I notice you don't have any children."

Margaret just shook her head.

The woman took a breath and then continued, "Well, in due time. At first, I hadn't wanted to bring children into this wild country either, but then, of course, I am very glad now to have my Jacob, Matthew, Jonathan, William, Charles, Samuel, and Abigail." She stopped to see Margaret's nod of approval.

"Sounds like a truly lovely family." Maggie hoped she sounded sincere.

"Oh yes, they are great children. The baby is Sammy." She suddenly stopped talking. "My husband, Drake, has gone out with some Rangers to see if they can rid the area of a few Comanches that are bothering folks. I hadn't want him to go, but you know how men are once they get a thought into their fool heads." Fear crept into the woman's voice. "Been gone now for about five days. That's why we didn't cross on our turn. We are waiting for Drake to return." The silence whipped around them. "I hope he is still alive out there." Her eyes looked beyond them, into the area that Margaret and Finn had just left behind.

Margaret put her hand gently on the woman's cheek. "I'm sure he will return soon."

The woman's eyes filled with glistening drops of clear liquid that hovered on the edges of her lower lids and then dropped silently down her round apple cheeks.

Margaret tried not to think about the eleven graves on the prairie with the small wooden crosses. She was grateful when a toddling boy grabbed his mother's skirt.

"Mama, Mama," the boy said.

Ida reached down and swung the little boy onto her hip. "And this is my little Sammy."

Margaret reached out her hand, and the little boy took her finger.

# CHAPTER TWELVE

Finn paid ten cents for her and Annabelle and another ten cents for his horse and himself, plus five more cents for Lizzy. He sold Patch's horse to a man who had just recently had to shoot his lame horse. *Patch would have approved,* he thought as he stared into the muddy red water.

Margaret stood next to Annabelle and watched the Red River splash up against the barge. Three days had passed, and their turn to cross the Red River had finally come.

He was standing on one side of the barge, and Margaret was on the other. Something changed in her after she'd had her bath and donned Ida's frock. She seemed lost in her own thoughts and sullen, not the Maggie he knew. He glanced toward her. She had her arm around Annabelle's neck and was staring north, the direction they had come, not toward where they were going.

Finn leaned on the rail and turned to look toward Texas. *Can't look back*, he thought. *Only got the day the good Lord has given me. Lookin' back doesn't get me anywhere.* He began to think of his da and his brothers. Lorcan would be there, acting superior as always. Finn smiled. *Well, he might be older than me, but I have a lot of experience under my belt now.* He thought of Tiernan, Keller, and little Carlin James. None of them were little boys any more, but when they got together, they argued and fought as if they were. He was looking forward to that.

His smile stayed on his face when he thought of how his mum had named each of them. Lorcan, the Little Warrior, Tiernan, the Little Lord, Keller, the Little Companion, and Carlin, the Little Champion. Finn's chest rose and fell with a chuckle. *All of them little, 'cept me! Me, I'm bright and fair. Had to be my copper-tinged hair. Why else would I escape being called little, too?* But the thought always perplexed him. All his brothers were little someones, and he was different. *Well, I am different.* He slapped his hand against the rail. *And it isn't just my darn hair!*

Margaret was lost in her own thoughts. *Eight days ago, Ida sent her husband off to fight Comanches. Now that poor woman is still there, waiting at Colbert's Crossing.*

Margaret watched Ida standing on the northern bank, waving her hand slowly back and forth. Margaret reluctantly raised her hand and waved back. She wanted to shout, *Leave, Ida! Just grab all your kids and leave. He's not coming back!* Oh, poor Ida, you just have so much hope. That Texas Ranger, Ross, sat up all night with you, filling your head, talking about how Rangers know how to hunt Indians and how your husband is going to be okay. Why did your stupid man leave you with all those babies to go and hunt Comanche? It doesn't make sense to me, she thought. Finn would do something dumb like that. He would want to go help his friends and comrades.

She looked across the barge at Finn. He had just slapped his hand on the rail. *Men. Thankfully, I don't have to deal with them once I am safely with my father in New Braunfels.*

A high-pitched female voice screamed on the landing, "He's coming! Margaret, my Drake is coming!" Ida jumped up and down on the edge of the river.

Maggie could barely hear the words, but she heard the unmistakable "Drake is coming." She placed her hands on her heart. "Oh, thank you, God, for answering my prayers." She waved frantically with both hands at Ida to let her know that she had indeed heard. She tried to holler back, "Ida, that's wonderful!" but the wind threw her voice back at her.

A sharp jolt shook Finn and Maggie as the barge landed. Finn nodded for Margaret to exit first. She led Annabelle over the planks and onto the earth once again. Margaret looked up as she felt a raindrop on her face. *So much for keeping Ida's dress clean*, she thought.

"Finn, did you hear Ida?"

He nodded. "Praise God. That man needed to come home to his family."

Maggie dropped her head. "I had no faith. I really thought the Comanches had killed him. I'm so ashamed, Finn. I just had no faith."

"It's understandable, Maggie. Sometimes we lose our faith a little while, and then God restores it in us. Faith's a gift, ya know. Pain makes us fall away. God understands these things."

She stared at Finn. He seemed different. "What now, Mr. Finn O'Cleary?" she asked as he joined her on land.

"We ride, Miss Margaret Mae Ditmar. We ride for about twenty days. We ride right up to your daddy's door." Finn mounted his horse and turned to follow a well-worn trail away from the barge.

Margaret followed closely behind on her beloved Annabelle. She thought about Ida, her husband Drake, and their children, and her whole body filled with joy. She tried not to think about Patch and the eleven crosses on the prairie. She tried not to think about Finn O'Cleary, but he was up there in front of her, leading the way. She tried desperately not to think about twenty more days on the trail.

She looked left and right at the changing foliage all around her. Autumn was coming. The golds and reds mixed beautifully with the greens. God had gone crazy with His paint-brush. A wild turkey ran in front of them, but Finn let it pass unharmed. They had plenty of food for the next few days.

Margaret already felt her saddle sores oozing. She thought stubbornly, *A woman's posterior was not meant to be tortured by a saddle!* The rain pelted her face and soaked Ida's dress until it was clinging uncomfortably to her chest and her legs. Finn didn't seem to mind the rain. He just kept his horse moving at a good pace, which forced little Annabelle to keep up. Margaret reached out and patted the little mule's neck. "Yer a good girl, Annabelle." As if in answer, the mule let out a whinny and a heehaw.

Rain fell for nineteen days straight. The rain wasn't delicate raindrops—no, it came down in torrents and sheets of water.

Finally, the sun came out, and their clothes began to dry. Margaret hung her bonnet from the saddle horn to dry. Her curls were all tangled and matted against her head. She had deep purple circles under her eyes from days with limited sleep. Sleeping was a difficult task when her bedclothes were squishy with rainwater. She never had said the words *How long before we arrive?* But when the mule came up to the side of Finn's horse, she looked up and, in a tired and scratchy voice, asked, "Finn, how much further now?"

He sighed heavily and answered with a voice that sounded just as weary as she was. "A day or so, that's all, Maggie. Just hang on. We're going to make it."

She nodded silently and spurred Annabelle to keep moving.

Finn seemed to become more and more distant as they neared their destination. He had spoken to her only to point out the moon and the stars, but that was as close as he came to communicating with her. Then, after days and days in the saddle, Finn and Margaret could see there in front of them, like a painted picture from a storybook, New Braunfels in the far distance. There were thirty-eight thousand Germans living in Texas, and ninety percent of them were living near New Braunfels.

They rode past houses of various sizes and materials, dotting the prairie. People came out of their doors waving. Some of them ran to them, bringing fruit or pies. They refused several requests that they stay and rest.

Prince Braunfels of Germany had bought five thousand square miles near San Angela in 1841, the year Margaret was born. Her father was one of the first six thousand German immigrants who had landed in Carlshafen in 1845. Margaret's uncontrolled painful thoughts rolled through her head. She tried to stop them, but the memories were too deeply etched:

*Mutter succumbed on the ship, the* Johan Detthart. She had dysentery. Margaret tried in vain to block her thoughts. She saw the body of her mother sliding over the ship's rail into the sea, and she heard the splash as her mother's body hit the water and then disappeared. She surveyed her father's blank face. Her father did not hug her or hold her. He had just lifted her up to look over the rail, just as he had done each morning of the long voyage, to watch the dead bodies slipping into the sea.

She remembered trying to call out, "Mutter." But her little voice caught in the wind. She watched her mother vanish and then felt her father's strong hands pull her tiny ones from his neck. Then he set her tiny feet back down on the wet, slippery deck. She could still hear his voice: "You are the lady of our house now, Margaret Mae," he had announced in his heavy German voice.

Finn glanced at Margaret and noticed that her cheeks were streaked with tears. He thought, *It's good to see Maggie so happy to be coming home to her da.* He felt a small squeeze in his chest, which he could not identify. Then the reality washed over him like a cold waterfall. *Soon, I will be saying goodbye to Margaret Mae Ditmar.*

The Ditmar home sat on a large knoll. It was a Greek revival with lush gardens, a chicken coop, a pig pen, a barn, and a corral filled with fine-looking steeds. They passed through a small herd of longhorns before they entered through a large gate into the main grounds of the house. Finn let the little mule pass him.

Margaret kicked Annabelle's sides, gently urging her to move more swiftly. As they got closer to the house, she saw an older man sitting on the huge porch in a rocking chair. She wasn't quite sure that he was her father until the mule stopped on the pathway up to the porch. She slid off the mule and stood next to the little beast, her hand resting on its side. Then she saw the man's eyes and his moustache. The man in the rocking chair was definitely her father.

She watched as the man slowly stood up. He snatched a rifle leaning against the porch. He, as always, was an imposing figure—about six feet four inches—and even more so with a rifle in his hand. Finn dismounted and went to Margaret's side when he saw the gun.

Margaret's father walked unhurriedly toward them and reached down and unlatched the gate. "Can I help you?" His eyes strained as he stared into Margaret's face. "Louisa?" His mind rushed with thoughts. He said, "Louisa is dead. You cannot be my Louisa." He waited a moment, and then he knew. "Margaret Mae. You are Margaret Mae."

"Yes, it's me, Vater. Your daughter." She waited for his arms to open wide to greet her, but his arms did not open. He kept them nailed to his sides.

"Margaret Mae is at Harriet Beecher Stowe's school for girls in Connecticut," he announced flatly.

"Yes, I was at school, Vater." Her eyes clouded. "*Ich bin zu Hause, Vater.* I'm home!"

"*Sie gehoren nicht hier,* Margaret Mae."

"But I *do* belong here, Vater! How can you say that? I am finally home!" Tears filled her eyes.

Margaret's tears fell down her cheeks. Finn wanted to reach out and place his palms on her cheeks once again to stop their flow, but he watched silently as the drops plunged down her cheeks and puddled in the neck of Ida's dress.

"I had to come home. I had to be with you, Vater."

Margaret's father shook his head. "No. This will not be."

Finn stepped forward. "Mr. Ditmar, if I may speak, sir?"

"Who are you, Irishman?" The old man had heard the Irish trill in the young man's words.

"I am the son of Keenan Michael O'Cleary. I am Finn Michael O'Cleary of Irish Flats." His posture straightened. "I have brought your daughter safely home, sir. She has had to endure a most treacherous and painful journey to come here. She had just one desire, good sir. Her only wish was to come home to her father. She is a tenacious woman, and she never gave up, even when it seemed, at times, that she couldn't travel another step. Sir, you cannot imagine what this dear woman has had to endure."

The German's voice turned to a raspy growl. "Margaret, did you travel alone with this man?"

"He is quite respectable, Vater. There were eleven other escorts, but they were killed by the Comanche." She wiped her face with the back of her hand and looked into his brown yellow- rimmed eyes. "Please," she pleaded, "I am home, Vater. Can't you be happy?"

The man twisted his moustache with his fingers before he spoke again. "Go to your room, Margaret Mae. It is the door at the top of the stairs. No daughter of mine travels with a man whilst she is unmarried."

"But Vater, you don't understand. Finn O'Cleary is an honorable man."

"We shall see about that, daughter. Go to your room!" His voice boomed.

A memory raced across Margaret's mind. *I'll hide behind Mutter's skirt, and he can't find me! I'll be safe. Mutter will keep me safe.* She shook her head as if doing so would knock the memory out of it. "Vater, please, you have to listen to me. I just wanted to be near you. We are family."

Her father turned and pointed to the double wooden doors leading into the house.

She glanced at Finn, who nodded toward her. She left him standing there with her father's hand poised on a rifle, held loosely at his side. As she mounted the polished wooden staircase, she remembered the ever-present Colt .44 strapped to Finn's side. A cold shiver ran up her spine.

Margaret's fathered stared at the young Irishman in front of him. Finn tried to address the German man again, "Sir, Mister Ditmar, sir, I assure you, the virtue of your daughter is entirely intact. There was no impropriety at any time."

The German man's brown eyes seemed to turn a shade of brownish amber. "Leave my land, Irishman, before I do something both of us will not like, though I doubt I would regret."

"Sir, I just want you to know that—"

"I beseech you to leave now, sir, while you can still ride. And take that stupid mule with you!"

"But, sir, this mule belongs to Miss Ditmar, and she's quite—"

"Take it!" The man roared. "And never step foot on my land again, do you hear me?"

"I do, sir. Yes, sir." Finn turned and grabbed the reins of the little mule and then mounted his own horse.

Finn O'Cleary rode swiftly out the gates, not looking back. He felt a hole in his heart, just as surely as if Hans Ditmar had shot him clean through. He kept his face straight forward and his jaw set, and he rode directly to Irish Flats, which was not far. Within an hour, he saw the tin roofs in the distance. It looked as if he was riding into Kilarney in Ireland. The O'Cleary house was in the middle of all of them. Finn thought of how long it had taken his father, his brothers, and him to finish the beautiful house. Da had wanted everyone to have their own rooms so the day they brought their brides home, there would be room for everyone.

His mind drifted to the days of sawing down the post oak for the front and back porches and making all the hewn logs just right so that they were flat on all sides. He shut his eyes for a moment as he remembered Lorcan yelling at him to get the half dove-tails "just right" when they made the wooden floor. Lorcan had made such a fuss. Da had smiled while they argued, and then Da finally had to break them apart as they rolled and punched at each other on the newly made floor.

Finn laughed aloud as he remembered the day. He hadn't allowed himself to think of any of his family for a long while. But he was almost home, and it was a luxury to let his mind drift to all his happy memories. Doing so would help block the memories of Margaret Mae Ditmar and her father.

He wrestled with his thoughts. *The woman doesn't need saving, Finn O'Cleary. She wanted her father, and now she has her father.* He looked up and saw his home. He noticed the green shutters were open, and he saw a flash of glass. *Why, I'll be! Da bought potato-starch glass windows!* As he got closer, he saw telltale bubbles in the glass.

He began to shout, "Da! Da! Lorcan! Tiernan! Keller! Carlin!" His voice was loud and clear. He knew they would all be there since it was later in the evening and they would all be home from working in the fields, probably sitting down to supper. "Da!" he hollered again. He slid off his horse when he saw Carlin James running toward him.

"Finn! Da, it's Finn!" The nineteen-year-old ran into the arms of his older brother and pounded his hands on his brother's back.

"You're home! You're finally home!" He yelled over his shoulder, "Da! It's Finn Michael! He's home! Oh, thank you, Jesus! I can't believe my eyes! You're home, Finn!"

A short, stocky man with a red face and thinning brown hair came bounding out the door, and it slammed behind him. "Boy! Oh, my boy! Thank the good Lord! You're back!" His father embraced him and kissed him on both cheeks. "Oh, yer a sight for my old eyes, Finn Michael O'Cleary!" His father kissed both his cheeks again. "Oh, praise the good Lord!"

"Da, where's Lorcan, Tiernan, and Keller?" Finn looked behind his father expectantly.

The old man shook his head, "Oh, boy, they are off getting ready for this civil war that's coming."

"What? What are you talking about?"

Carlin James spoke for his father. "The brothers are going to join the Union if war breaks out, so they thought they should head out east. They left right after you did, Finn. They had read about John Brown's raid at Harper's Ferry in Virginia, and well, they just made up their minds and left. You know how the brothers are."

"Joined the Union? Are they abolitionists now?"

His father nodded. "They be the righteous ones, Finn Michael." His father stared into his son's face. "Ah, you always have had the angel face of your dear ma, Finn Michael O'Cleary. I see her eyes. I see her smile." He reached out and hugged his son again. "So good to have you home, son. I am blessed by the good Lord to have my lost sheep returned."

"Da, I wasn't lost. I was on a cattle drive, and I made some good money." He grinned. "But I see you must've come into some doubloons yerself with those new glass windows."

Keenan O'Cleary laughed a deep warm laugh. "Can't say things have been too bad, Son. I just miss your brothers. I put them in the good Lord's hands. I know He will bring them back to me, just like he has you." He hugged Finn again and laid his head against his son's chest. His head came right under Finn's chin. "Come on in, son. Supper's waiting."

Finn sat in his customary chair at the long table and looked at all the empty seats, where he normally would have seen the mischievous faces of his brothers. Little Carlin James sat next to his da's elbow, as always, but he felt as if he was sitting at a ghost table without his brothers' laughter.

His father saw the distant look in his blue eyes. "I know, son. The table is not quite noisy enough. I feel it, too. But your brothers felt that they had to do what's right. They felt inspired by God to right the wrongs. I am of the same mind, son. No man should own another. But if the Lord is willin', we all will be together again. Eat up, son. Then we'll talk about the trail drive."

Finn put down his fork. "Da, Patch was killed by Comanche."

His father made the sign of the cross. "Jesus, Joseph, Mary, God give him peace."

"Da, that's not all. All of them are gone. All eleven of them dead."

Keenan O'Cleary pushed his plate away. "All the boys are dead? We need to ride to their mothers."

Finn dropped his head. "Yes. I don't want to, Da, but we must."

"But yer here to tell the tale, son. How's that?" A frightened thought crossed the old man's mind. *Had my brave son run away? Is my boy a coward?*

"Da, I was hired to bring a young woman to her father in New Braunfels. She and I were riding further back on the trail. Ya see, she was on a mule on account of she doesn't know how to ride a horse. By the grace of God, I am here to tell you that I wish I had been with Patch that day."

His father slowly got out of his chair, came around the table, and put his hand firmly on Finn's shoulder. "Thank God you weren't, son. God knew best. What's the young woman's name?"

"Margaret Mae Ditmar. I call her Maggie." He turned to look at his father. "She's a wildcat, Da. Knows her own mind, and she was educated in one of those eastern girls' schools. She is the most exasperating woman I have ever met. I kept wishing you had told me about women, Da. I just didn't know what to do with her tantrums and her..." He stopped, remembering her tears. "And her horrid tears. They just pour out of her eyes like some burstin' rain cloud."

His father laughed. "You love 'er, don't you, son?"

"Good Lord, no! I want to wring her little chicken neck! And I thought beeves were stubborn. She is the most..."

"Finn Michael O'Cleary, you know I always know when you are fibbin'." His father's eyes were twinkling. "Looks like we are going to have our first wedding in the O'Cleary family."

"Da! It isn't like that! She's German, and she's prissy, and the worst, Da, the very worst, is that she's a Protestant."

His father reacted as if he had told him that she'd been spawned from hell. His father's face drained of its ruddy complexion and turned white. He slowly pulled out his chair, which was next to Finn, the one where Keller usually sat, and he sat down. The man spoke slowly and deliberately. "Then this is a grave matter, Finn Michael O'Cleary. Very grave indeed. We can take it up with the Lord and Father Timothy O'Brian. He will know what you should do. You aren't the first in St. Patrick's County that's fallen in love with a Protestant. Yer dear mother, Mary Katherine, God rest her dear soul, would be disappointed if we didn't give love a chance, but since our history is a bit convoluted, since coming here from Lurgan, Armagh County, we aren't too keen on Protestants."

"But, Da, I don't love Maggie Ditmar."

"Uh huh." He put his arm around his son's shoulders, "We'll work it out, boy. That's all yer ol' da can say. Nothing is impossible when you ask the good Lord's help."

# CHAPTER THIRTEEN

Each rock Finn tossed missed its mark. He was puffing heavily as he heaved them toward the window. "Maggie Mae!" he whisper-yelled. Finally, after several rocks missed their mark, two hit the window panes.

Margaret opened the sash. "What are you doing, Finn O'Cleary. My father will kill you if he finds you here! Are you crazy?"

"Maybe. Nope, I don't think so. I know my mind. Margaret Mae Ditmar. Will you marry me?"

"You're drunk, Finn! Go away!" She whisper-yelled back at him.

"I'm coming up, Maggie."

"No, Finn! Wait. I'll come down. Be quiet, or Father will hear you! Promise me you won't make a sound." She leaned out the window, her honey-brown hair was shimmering in the candlelight.

"I promise to wait right here if you hurry."

Maggie didn't wait but closed the window, ran to her dressing area, and changed her gown. She wrapped a ribbon around her hair and tiptoed down the winding stairs. *Thank goodness Father is in his study*, she thought as she opened the heavy front door. She ran onto the porch, where Finn had his arms wide open.

"Give us a hug, Maggie Mae."

"You are crazy, Finn. My father has a rifle, and he will use it."

Finn pulled aside his long coat. "And I also have a gun, my Colt. But Maggie, I'm here for only one thing." He fell onto one knee. "Will you be my wife, Margaret Mae Ditmar? That's all I came here to know."

She looked into his blue eyes, lit by the moon. His broad smile brought out his dimples. His clothes were washed and pressed. His hair was combed.

"You're not drunk at all, are you?" she asked.

He shook his head. "Definitely not. I have not had a drop of whiskey since I dropped you off here with your cold-hearted Da three weeks since. Three long miserable weeks without your smile, Maggie." He reached for her hand. "I love you, Maggie. God help me, I do. Will you marry me?" He looked up into her face. *Jesus, Mary, and Joseph, she is dangerously pretty.*

She shook her head as her curls tumbled down the front of her gown. "You know I can't. You must ask my father."

"No, Maggie, I am asking you." His voice was stern. "Only you. Then, we will go to Father O'Brian, and he will marry us. Quiet-like. You and me and Da and my brother Carlin alone there in St. Mary's Church." He squeezed her hand. "Won't you please marry me, Miss Margaret Mae Ditmar?" He looked up and saw the full moon glowing behind her head.

"I-I..." she stammered.

His eyes were liquid pools, oceans of aqua, glistening with merriment. She turned to look at her father's big house, with a gas lamp lit on the porch. "Maggie, you know you love me. You know it."

She glanced at Annabelle waiting for her in the yard. "You brought Annabelle," she whispered.

"I did indeed. She's missed you."

"Oh, and I have missed her, too."

He shook his head, "She and I should never have left you here with that monster."

"Finn! That monster is my father." She raised her voice.

"He doesn't deserve a beautiful daughter such as you. Answer me, Maggie. I can't wait another second. Will you marry me?"

She turned her palms up. "Now?"

"Is that a yes?" He stood up, his face inches from hers. He put both of his hands firmly on her waist. "Maggie, there is no one I want to be with for the rest of my life. No one else I want to bear my children and raise them with. Only you, Maggie." He ran the back of his fingers down her cheek. "There is no one I want to greet each morning and bid good night to each night, other than you." He leaned in until she could feel his breath against her lips. "I didn't know, Maggie. I didn't know how much I would miss your smile, the light in your eyes. I didn't know that I fell in love with you." He shook his head slowly. "No, I knew. I knew that day I lay next to you under that stagecoach. I knew, but I wouldn't let myself believe it. I wanted to roll you over and hold you tight in my arms forever and keep you safe. I knew right then, Maggie, right under that stagecoach." He picked up one of her curls on her shoulder and felt the smoothness of it between his fingers. "I don't know what else to say, my dearest. I am in great pain here. I feel broken without you. I..."

She put the palm of her hands on his chest. "I love you too, Finn Michael O'Cleary. The answer is yes. I will marry you."

He heard a loud *boom* and felt something flying through the air, whizzing past his right leg.

"Get away from my daughter, you Irish scoundrel!"

Finn heard another booming sound, but he had already started to run, and the bullet missed its mark. He had grabbed Maggie's hand, but she wriggled it out of his grasp.

"Run, Finn! Run, my love! I'll be safe! You need to run!" She saw him leap for his horse, grabbing Annabelle's reins as he flew into the saddle. With a sharp kick of his boots, the three of them bounded down the trail with Finn on his horse and the little mule running behind as fast as her stubby legs could go.

Margaret turned toward her father. His eyes were the deepest golden color she had ever seen them turn.

He held the rifle in the crook of his arm. His dark-blue velvet smoking jacket was buttoned across his barrel-like chest. He glared at her. "You... you...!" He sputtered, his thick spit flying into the air. "You are not my daughter! You will go back to Harriet Beecher Stowe's school for women. You will become a teacher and spend the rest of your days as a spinster schoolmarm."

His voice was so loud that she felt Finn could hear him even as he escaped down the trail. She lifted her skirt, slowly and unhurriedly. She calmly turned her back to him and started toward the front door.

He bellowed at her, "Do you understand me, Margaret Mae Ditmar?"

She opened the big, heavy front door and went into the house.

His voice was still thundering in the yard. "*Verstehst du mich, Tochter?*"

She climbed the stairs quickly. Silently, she answered him, *Yes, Father. I understand you very clearly.* She threw some of her gowns into a small carrying bag. She draped a black cape over her shoulders. She thought, *I know Finn will be waiting for me.* Quickly, she ran down the stairs with the bag held tightly in her hand. She pushed open the door and saw her father standing there, like the gigantic Red River raft jam. She thrust her bag into his side as she pushed past him. "Out of my way." She bolted down the pathway.

He continued to rant. "I will not be disgraced by you, Margaret Mae Ditmar! I will not have my blood daughter cavorting with Irishmen!" He raised his rifle and steadied it on his bent arm.

She kept scampering away from the house. Her thoughts swam through her mind, bumping into each other in her head, not making any sense as she ran.

"Stop, daughter! Halt! I am your father! You must obey! Halt!" The old man's finger quivered on the trigger. He squeezed slowly. The bullet whizzed past Margaret's head, missing its mark. She dropped her bag and ran even faster, faster than she had ever run in her life.

She saw the silhouette of Finn's horse hiding in a thicket and ran toward it. "Finn! Finn!" When she reached the horse, the saddle was empty. Annabelle was standing by quietly. She looked around the area and whispered, "Finn?" There was no answer.

Finn couldn't hear her. Finn lay on his stomach in the high grass. He had heard the gunshots, but he was still too far away to help

Maggie. He inched his way closer to the house, scraping his belly through the rocks and dirt. He could see the old man clearly, his rifle still in his hand, his golden eyes scanning the night air.

He screamed, "Margaret! Come back here! I will hunt you down, Margaret Mae, and I will kill you and your lover!" He turned slowly in a half circle and then peered toward the thicket.

Finn thought the old man could see him, but he just kept glowering.

"I will come for you, Margaret! I will find you! Make no mistake. You cannot hide from me." He bellowed even louder. "You will not disgrace me! There is no place you can hide! I am an honorable man!"

Finn continued to move closer, slithering like a Texas coral snake, closer and closer. He could see the old man's golden eyes peering straight at him, but Finn was under a pile of leaves, ten feet away from the barrel of the old man's gun.

He knew the old man would see the flash of the Colt's barrel if he tried to shoot him from that distance. Finn carefully slid his knife out of his belt and placed it in his teeth. **More 'n one way to skin an alligator.** He waited for the moment, holding his breath. The man looked away when he heard a noise at the end of the path. Finn jumped out and tackled the big man to the ground. He threw the rifle into the bushes and punched Hans Ditmar's face over and over again. He sat on the old German's hard, rounded belly and kept pummeling his face with his fists.

The man's face began to bleed profusely. "Get off of me! Get off of me, you Irish swine!" The German's big hands grabbed for Finn's hair and held on. He shook Finn's head back and forth, left to right, trying to throw the younger man off his chest. He stared into Finn's eyes, which were like daggers looking over the blade caught firmly in his teeth.

Finn at once took the knife from his mouth and placed the blade against the old man's throat.

Ditmar bellowed in his thick German accent, "Do it! Do it! I dare you to cut the neck of your future wife's father. Margaret will hate you forever." He began to laugh, a hysterical, deep belly laugh. "Yes, Irish scoundrel, you will be killing your father-in-law. Can you live with it, you Papist little swine?"

Finn kept the knife on the man's throat. "I can do this," he said aloud. "You hurt her. You hurt Margaret terribly. You kept your love from her!"

Hans Ditmar hollered even more loudly, "She is strong! Margaret Mae is not weak like her mother. She is a survivor. I made her a survivor. Me. I made her survive." The old man's goldish-brown eyes were changing, returning to brown. His eyes no longer made him appear as if he was a crazed animal. "Her mother left me alone to raise a girl. What do I know of a daughter? She didn't even live long enough to give me my son!" His voice became a whine. "She just was so weak, so frail. She couldn't finish the journey. She died, leaving me with Margaret. She took my son with her into her watery grave!" The old man's eyes began to fill with tears. "What could I do? How could I raise a child? How could I raise a daughter?"

Hans Ditmar looked up and saw Margaret standing above him, holding his own rifle pointed at his head. His voice softened. "Margaret, I didn't know what I should do with a daughter all by myself. I sent you away to school to make a strong woman of you, so you wouldn't be like your mother. Do you understand?"

Margaret kept her eyes on him, holding the gun steady. "Get off of him, Finn."

Finn stood up, and they both looked down at the old man. Margaret started to squeeze the trigger slowly. "You miserable old man. You tried to kill me. You tried to kill me! Your own flesh and blood!"

Finn whispered, "Don't do it, Maggie. It's cold-blooded murder. Don't do it." He put his hand on hers. "Let's get out of here, Maggie. Come on, now. Leave the old fool to die alone."

Maggie ran her finger over the trigger as if she were petting Annabelle's throat.

She looked into her father's glazed eyes, her voice flat and drained of emotion. "You lifted me up to the ship's rail each morning to see all that death! You made me watch all those dead people fall into the sea—me, a little, innocent child."

"I wanted you to be strong. I wanted you to be brave, Margaret." He turned his face away from her, "I was wrong. I was very, very wrong."

Finn put his arm around Maggie's shaking shoulders, "Come on, Maggie. Let's go to St. Mary's. Father O'Brian is waiting for us. I told him we would come if he would do it."

"You are going to marry this Catholic?" The German spat on the ground as he sat up.

She nodded. "Yes, Father. I am going to marry Finn Michael O'Cleary, and I am proud to do so. He's a good man, father. He's fair and just and—"

"And I love her," Finn added. "I love her with my whole heart and soul." He squeezed her shoulders. "Put the gun down, Maggie. Let's go."

She dropped the rifle and let Finn guide her back to where his horse and Annabelle were waiting patiently.

He lifted her onto Annabelle's back. "All set? It's not far. We'll be there before morning."

She nodded silently as she nudged Annabelle's sides with her satin-slippered feet. Annabelle followed behind, as she had done for hundreds of miles.

As soon as he saw the house, Finn shouted for his father. "Da! Da!"

Keenan O'Cleary hurried out, with Carlin James right behind him. "So here she is!" The Irishman's blue eyes were sparkling, lit up by the smile on his face. "Hello, darlin'. I'm your da." He reached up and lifted Margaret off Annabelle's back. "We've been waiting for you all night." He kissed her on each of her cheeks. "Aren't you the mornin's glory? So beautiful!"

Finn jumped off his horse. "This is Margaret Mae, Da. I call her Maggie."

"So then, Maggie it is!" He hugged Maggie's shoulders tightly.

"Please to meet you, Mr. O'Cleary." She could barely find her voice.

"Mister, is it? Oh, no no no. I am your da, and that is that." He put both his warm hands on her cheeks. "You are such a delight to my eyes, Maggie, and will be the light in our home! Come. Come with me." He grabbed her hand and led her back toward the house but bumped into Carlin. "Oh, and this is your brother, Carlin James."

Carlin smiled timidly. "Pleased to meet you, Maggie." He reached out and hugged her. "I am filled with joy at having a sis. I am sure the other brothers will be most pleased to be your brothers, too."

Keenan O'Cleary pushed his hand against the small of her back. "Come into the house, Maggie my girl! We have to hurry. The sun is coming up, and Father O'Brian is waiting for us."

"Da, what are you doing?" Finn asked. "We have to go."

"Not yet. Not yet, son. Maggie and I have to have a little talk. Come with me, girl." He turned to Finn. "And you wait in the parlor, Finn O'Cleary."

He pulled on her hand and led her to a back bedroom. There on a four-poster bed was a white gown. It had been carefully smoothed out. "It was Finn's mum's. She wore it on our wedding day. I'd be mighty pleased if you wanted to wear it today, Maggie."

Maggie reached out her hand and gently touched the silk gown. "It's so lovely," she whispered.

"And the veil is silk, too, with those little pearls that my wife, Mary Katherine, loved so much." He reached out and touched a pearl with a fingertip. "I'll leave you now to dress, and then we can go to St. Mary's Church." He stepped back and took her tiny hands in his weathered, callused ones. "You will be a beautiful bride, Maggie. Finn has made a wise choice, and I am most pleased to give you both my blessing." He turned and left her there to dress.

When she had put the dress on, combed her curls, and set the veil with the seed pearls adorning its halo on her head, she went back into the parlor.

Finn gasped when he saw her. "You are..." He stopped and shook his head. "I don't have the words, Maggie. You are an angel on earth. That's what you are."

"Enough! Off to the church," Da said. "The sun is up, and it's time. Father O'Brian will be waiting!" He hurried them out the door.

Carlin had brought the buggy around the front of the house. It wasn't a polished, fancy buggy, but it had a cover and cushioned seats. He helped her into the seat, rolling her gown around his arms so as not to let it drag in the dust.

"You're not to go with us, brother." Carlin smiled at Finn. "You and Da will ride on the horses." He took the reins, and they traveled to St. Mary's.

Father O'Brian was indeed waiting on the steps. He had his service robes on and a prayer book folded against his chest. "Hello, hello. You must be the chosen bride of Finn Michael."

Maggie nodded.

"You are a vision, young lady, a true vision. What is your given name?"

"Margaret Mae."

"Fine, fine. You shan't be married on the altar, you not being a Catholic and all, but do you desire to practice the faith of your future husband?"

Margaret glanced at Finn, who was looking at her with that frown that she had come to know as his "worry brow." She whispered, "Yes."

"And you will be raising your children in the Catholic Church?"

Maggie nodded.

"Come with me, children." They followed Father O'Brian into the church. It was cool and smelled of incense. Candles flickered on the altar.

She had never been in a Catholic church before. Her eyes darted to the statue of the Blessed Mother holding the infant Jesus.

Father O'Brian took her hand. "Kneel here, child."

Maggie knelt on the cold white marble.

"Kneel beside her, Finn Michael."

Finn knelt next to her and glanced at her face to make sure she wasn't turning white from fear, but her eyes were fixed straight ahead. She was looking at the crucifix on the altar.

"You may take Margaret Mae's hand." The priest smiled as he stood in front of the kneeling bride and groom.

"Who gives this woman to this man?"

Da cleared his voice. "I, Keenan Michael O'Cleary, in proxy for her father, Hans Ditmar, do give this woman to this man."

"Who stands for this man?"

Carlin James nodded. "I, Carlin James, the brother of Finn Michael, stand for this man as representative of all of the brothers, Keller, Tiernan, and Lorcan."

"Do you, Margaret Mae, take Finn Michael to be your lawful husband, to have and to hold from this day forward, for better, for worse, for richer, for poorer, in sickness and health, until death do you part?"

"I do."

"Do you, Finn Michael, take Margaret Mae to be your wife and promise to be true to her in good times and in bad, in sickness and in health, and will you honor and love her all the days of your life?"

Finn turned toward her. "I do."

Father O'Brian placed one hand on Maggie's head and one hand on Finn's head. "In Jesus' name, I bless Finn Michael and Margaret Mae as husband and wife from this day forward, in the name of the Father, the Son, and the Holy Ghost. What God has joined together, let no man take apart. You are husband and wife. Finn Michael, you may kiss your wife."

Finn stood, reached down, and pulled Maggie up by her hands. He lifted her veil so he could see her cocoa-brown eyes, reflections of the candles dancing in them. He put his hand under her chin and tilted her head up toward him. For a moment, he stared at her soft pink lips, those lovely full lips he had wanted to kiss for so many days. He whispered, "I love you, Mrs. O'Cleary." He leaned down and pressed his lips against hers. His head began to spin, and his stomach felt as if he and his horse had leaped over a hedge at top speed.

Stretched up on her tippy toes, she leaned into his kiss. Her eyes were closed, but she could smell his warm scent, that same scent she had smelled when he had held her close under the stagecoach.

Keenan O'Cleary sniffed loudly. "Daughter!" He pulled her away from Finn and hugged her tightly. "Welcome to the family."

Carlin grinned and nodded toward her, but she reached out and took his hand, leaning into him and forcing him to hug her.

Finn reached for her hand and pulled her close. He wrapped his arm around her as they walked out of the church.

Father O'Brian stayed in the church. He sat down in the front pew, staring at the cross on the altar. "Lord, be with them and watch over them and bless them with many healthy children." He bowed his head. "I know I did the right thing, Lord, in your eyes. I don't know what Bishop Odin will think, but that is a matter for another day."

Finn helped Maggie into the buggy. He jumped up and sat next to her. He put his arm around and pulled her in close. "I love you, Maggie. I truly do. I will be a good husband. I promise you that."

She placed her hand lightly on his thigh. "I know you will, Finn Michael."

Carlin rode his brother's horse. The little wedding party headed back to the farmhouse with Da and Carlin leading the way.

Maggie leaned into Finn's shoulder and whispered into his ear, "And I will be a good wife, and we will have many sons."

His eyes locked onto hers as he pulled tightly up on the reins to stop the buggy. He yanked her tightly against his chest. "I've been wanting to kiss you proper from the first day I met you, Maggie." He pressed his lips against hers, grinding his moist lips into hers with a craving to brand her as his forever.

Chloe Emile

# ABOUT THE AUTHOR

Chloe Emile writes sweet, clean romance, whether it's contemporary or historical. She can usually be found working on her next novel, eating takeout with her husband, or watching rom-coms.

**www. ChloeEmile.com**

*Finn*

Chloe Emile